The Crystal Lair

Inventor-in-Training,

Book Two

D.M. Darroch

Illustrations by Jennifer L. Hotes

SLEEPY CAT PRESS

Copyright text © 2013 by D.M. Darroch
Copyright illustrations and cover image © 2013 by Jennifer L. Hotes

ISBN-10: 1-890797-09-X
ISBN-13: 978-1-890797-09-6

To Aidan and Matt

A Note to My Readers

I want to remind my faithful readers that I, your author, am a storyteller, not a scientist. While I did copious research for *The Crystal Lair*, I strongly urge any inventors-in-training to visit your local natural science museums, ask your librarians and science teachers for guidance, and speak with geologists, anthropologists, and paleontologists before attempting any lab work of your own.

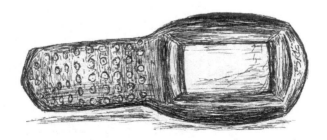

You never know into which world a scientific mishap will send you.

Contents

1

In a Frozen World

The day Angus Clark transported himself to a snowy wasteland didn't begin like any other mundane day in his previously mundane life.

Ever since he had built the Insect Incinerator that had turned out to be a World Jumper, nothing in his life was routine. First, he had accidentally transported himself to a pirate world. He had survived a crew of nasty pirates who had stolen the invention that was his only way back home. He'd only had time to make a few adjustments to his World Jumper before having another accident. Now, he was in yet another world completely surrounded by icy whiteness.

Angus Clark was an inventor-in-training. He still had a lot to learn before becoming a full-fledged inventor.

Angus brushed snow from the front of his shirt and jeans. His jump across worlds had landed him face down in a snow pile. He gazed about in curiosity and wonder. He stood on a large plateau. To his left a grove of evergreen trees sloped gently downward toward a thick forest. Above him a blue sky was beginning to darken as clouds moved in. In the distance, to his right, a rocky outcropping grew into foothills. He turned around slowly, his feet crunching and compressing the snow.

"Ivy!" he called. "Ivy! Are you here?" There was no response. "Yoo-hoo! Anyone? Anyone here?" He heard nothing but the wind whistling through the trees.

The sky grew darker.

Lazy flakes began to fall from the sky. Angus felt them melt as they touched the top of his head. He took inventory. Toolbelt wrapped securely around waist. Check. Trusty screwdriver in toolbelt. Check. Safety goggles atop head. Check. World Jumper? Tucked into waistband of jeans. He'd have to find a more secure spot for it.

Angus loved snow, though he didn't get much opportunity to play in it at home. It didn't snow often in the Puget Sound area near Seattle and when it did the snow melted quickly. Angus shared a love of snow with his father. In the winter Mr. Clark frequently took Angus to the mountains. Father and son spent many happy hours together skiing the slopes. In fact, Angus liked skiing so much he had attempted to build a ski slope in the family backyard.

Angus's yard boasted a glorious hill. It was not quite black diamond quality, but a blue square slope in a suburban community is nothing to scoff at. The problem was, as stated before, it didn't often snow in the Puget Sound area. Rain was quite abundant in the winter however. And as any self-respecting boy knows, where there's rain, there's plenty of slippery stuff. That is, mud.

Mrs. Clark had told him she'd only be at the neighbor's house for a half-hour or so. But his mother's conversations tended to drag on as he knew from painful experience. He was sure she'd probably said, "Oh, but I really should go. Angus is all alone at home," at least four times before she finally left. But it was okay because Angus was not home alone after all. In fact, quite a few of his best buddies from the neighborhood were with him. Together they had managed to create two respectable runs and one bunny slope before his mother returned from her "short" visit.

The guys were having a great time. They were mogul racing and ski jumping. There was a lively contest to see who could wipe out in most spectacular fashion. Billy Roberts had started a mudball war that Angus was winning when Mrs. Clark returned. The vein throbbing in his mother's temple was Angus's first indication he was in trouble. Shortly thereafter, angry neighborhood mothers arrived to retrieve their mud-caked sons from The Slopes at Clark House. Angus's skis were held ransom by Mrs. Clark for the rest of that winter. Now, whenever Mr. Clark mows over the former moguls, he scalps the lawn.

The sky had turned a leaden gray and the snow was falling more quickly now. Angus shivered and hugged himself. He knew this cold fluffy stuff could turn deadly if he wasn't dressed for it. He was still wearing his shirt and jeans from home. He had no hat, jacket, or gloves. The purple rhinestone sneakers he'd found in the pirate world were already caked with melting snow. He would need to find clothing or shelter soon. And, since there was nothing around him but snow and trees, it wasn't going to be clothing.

He considered his survival options.

He could hunker down in the trees. They would provide some shelter from the coming storm but they wouldn't keep him warm.

He could gather wood and try to start a fire. There were sure to be plenty of sticks and flammable detritus in the forest but, even if he could get the wet wood to catch fire, the falling snow would surely extinguish it.

He could explore the rocky foothills for a sheltered space where he could start a fire. The rocks would hold and magnify the fire's heat but it would be a bit of a trudge through the snow to get there. Again, he might not manage to get the wood to catch fire.

He could curl up with a furry mammal and live off its body heat. If only Ivy were here! She could jump into something warm and cuddly and he could wear her like a coat.

Angus missed Ivy. In his home world, Ivy Calloway was the perfect student. She was good at everything and not afraid to let you know it. All the teachers loved her. Her assignments were always neat and handed in on time. She was the first one they called on; she always knew the answers, she never daydreamed in class, and she always had her pencils. You know, the perfect nightmare classmate for the student who gets lost in his own head, forgets project deadlines, and has terrible handwriting. A student like Angus. And wouldn't it just figure that Ivy was in every one of his classes.

But the Ivy Calloway Angus had met in the pirate world was, if not the best friend any inventor-in-training could have, pretty near to it. Sure, she was every bit as sharp-tongued and know-it-all as the Ivy in Angus's world, but she was also loyal, brave, funny, and smart. And she was a body jumper, which made her exceptionally awesome.

Ivy was a potions expert. Well, maybe expert was overstating it a bit. After all, she'd had an accident with one of her potions in much the same way that Angus had an accident with his invention. She had drunk one of her own potions and been somehow removed from her own body. She now jumped from animal body to animal body trying to find a way to get back to her human body. Now she and Angus were a team and hoped that, together, they could find a way back to their respective worlds and bodies.

"Iiiivyyy! Iiiivyyy!" Angus called again. He hoped she would be able to find him. He had left the pirate world a bit hastily. He didn't know whether or not she'd be able to catch up with him.

Angus jumped up and down to get the blood moving in his feet. He shook his arms and flapped them back and forth across his body. He was going to freeze to death if he didn't make a decision soon. He plodded through the wet snow toward the grove of trees. The boughs over his head intertwined, weaving their needles together like children holding hands. Angus was able to find broken sticks, small punky logs, and leaf and needle litter lightly dusted with snow. He gathered what he could in his pockets, stuffed twigs in his toolbelt, and grabbed as many logs as he could carry.

Just then he remembered something he had seen on one of those wilderness survival programs his dad was so fond of watching on Saturday afternoons. The survival guy had layered dry leaves and peat moss on the floor of his shelter to insulate against damp and cold. These trees were covered with moss. Why not try insulating himself?

He dropped the logs, pulled his trusty screwdriver from his toolbelt, and began scraping the moss off the trees. He removed one purple sneaker at a time and stuffed the moss inside. The sneakers had been too big and the moss helped them fit a bit snugger. His toes curled around the soft plant material. He tied the sneakers tightly and then pushed moss up his pant leg as far as he could reach.

He unzipped his jeans and crammed moss into them from the top. He tucked his shirt into the jeans, scraped more moss off another tree, and packed his shirt with it. He was absolutely rotund now but no longer felt so cold. After some deliberation he decided to head for the foothills.

He thought he'd have a better chance of finding shelter among the rocks than in the damp forest. He picked up the logs again and set off across the plateau.

While Angus had been insulating himself, the wind had picked up. It blew the fine grains of snow hard against his face. They burned like fire as they struck him, and then his cheeks were numb. He bent his head low against the onslaught and kept going. He lost sensation in his ears and his fingers. He hugged the logs to his chest with his forearms and continued on, one laborious step after another through the heavy, wet snow.

His arms ached from the weight of the logs. His legs ached from struggling through the snow. His head ached from the cold. "One, two, three," he began counting each step. He needed to focus on his forward progress and get his mind off his sore body. He kept counting until his foot nudged something hard at one thousand six hundred and twenty-five. He stopped walking and glanced up. He'd bumped into a small boulder, the beginning of the foothills.

In front of him were rocks of every size piled up the side of a large hill. He walked to a large boulder with a flat top and unloaded his logs. He wandered around the side of the hill looking for a rock overhang under which he might shelter and build a fire. Rock after snow-covered rock, boulder on top of boulder. He needed to find a place soon.

Puffy-full of moss and clumsy-numb with cold, Angus tripped over his own feet, landed hard on a boulder, and knocked the wind out of himself. He groaned and gasped for air.

And then he saw it.

An oblong opening about the size of the small bathroom window in his family's house was carved into the side of the hill. He never would have found it if he hadn't stumbled. It was hidden by the boulder on which he had fallen. He would have to scramble over the boulder into a crevice in the side of the hill and then sideways into the opening.

If Ivy had been with him, she would have warned him to wait a moment, think about what he was about to do, and consider whether or not it was safe. But Ivy wasn't with him. Angus rolled across the boulder and scooted himself into the gap.

The opening was wide enough but low to the ground. He got down on his knees and crawled in expecting a small cavity perfect for hunkering down in or perhaps a narrow tunnel where he could stretch his legs. His mind raced considering where best to build his fire. But when he had passed through the gap into the dark recesses of the hill, he realized he could raise his head. He carefully lifted his hands over his head and stood. His fingers touched air. He slowly spread his hands outward to his waist.

He had expected to encounter a rock wall but he felt nothing. Arms stretched straight out, Angus slowly turned in a half-circle until he was facing the aperture. His body no longer blocked the opening and daylight pierced through the darkness. Sure that he could find the exit if need be, Angus backed away from the entry and completed his circle rotation. He rooted around in his toolbelt until his fingers located his pen flashlight. He had to use it sparingly. He didn't know when he'd arrive at a world with batteries. He flicked it on.

Light glinted off the ceiling and walls. The ceiling of the cave, for it was indeed a cave that Angus had crawled into, rose gradually from the crevice he had entered to a high point of about twelve feet. The interior was illuminated with all the colors of the rainbow. Forgetting how cold he was for a moment, Angus tripped to a wall and brushed it with a finger. The entire cave was encrusted with beautiful crystals of every conceivable color: white, purple, blue, green, yellow, orange, red, and pink. He had never seen anything like this. And as a Junior Rock Hounder, he knew a lot about rocks.

Angus had been an early stone aficionado. From a young age he had gathered pebbles, stones, and other hard shiny objects in his pockets and shoes. Several times he had smuggled rocks home from a friend's gravel driveway in his mother's purse. He would lie in the grass, specimens scattered around him as he searched for them in identification guides. Occasionally, he forgot a few and they would be found a few days later, with clanging and smoke, by his father's lawnmower. The appliance repairman had suggested the Junior Rock Hounders as a suitable outlet for Angus's fascination the third time Angus's mother called him after forgetting to check her son's jean pockets on laundry day.

Angus fastened his safety goggles securely over his eyes, took a small chisel and hammer from his toolbelt, and carefully chipped away at the wall until he was able to extract several of the variously colored crystals. He examined them closely. They were cubes and octahedrons. He peered at the wall again and saw several that were colorless. He chipped a particularly large one from the wall, held it to his eye and peered through it. It was clear like glass.

He shone his penlight through the clear crystal. As he'd suspected, there was zero light scatter inside the crystal. He had discovered a cave full of fluorite. He flicked off the light to conserve his battery. The light from the cave's opening reflected gently off the crystal-encrusted walls giving Angus the impression that he was surrounded by tiny night lights.

Angus gazed at the stones in his hand and looked up at the wall again. As a Junior Rock Hounder, he knew that fluorite was a fairly common mineral found in large deposits around the world. But he'd never heard of the existence of so many color veins in one small area. He pulled the sticks out of his pocket to make room for his collection of crystals. The sticks dropped to the floor. In his wonderment, Angus had forgotten completely about the fire he was planning to build.

He pushed the goggles to the top of his head, clumping his unruly hair into a messy pile. Angus dragged his fingers along the bumpy, glittering wall and slowly walked the perimeter of the chamber.

The dim light of the cave's opening barely reached the farthest corners of the cave. Angus thought he noticed some hair, or perhaps fur, clinging to the cubic crystals at shoulder level. He clicked on the small flashlight again and gathered the fur in his hand. It was a brownish color with flecks of gold and red.

He shone the flashlight on the wall and saw clumps of the fur scratched off in a horizontal line. He followed the line along the wall and detected a collection of grass, leaves, and fur at the entrance of what appeared to be a narrow passageway at the rear of the cave.

Was it a trick of the light or did he see something move in there? He bent to get a closer look.

"Gus! GUS! GUSSSEEEE!" screeched in his ear and he was shoved from behind. His flashlight skittered to the hard cave floor as he lost his balance and fell to his knees.

2

Extended Family

Angus quickly retrieved his flashlight from the floor before trying to remove the rapidly breathing thing that was clinging to his back. He couldn't see it, but it was furry and warm and strong. He grabbed the paws that dug into his shoulders and pulled back on them as hard as he could to make them release him.

"OWWWWW!" The animal dropped away.

Angus spun around and caught sight of a small furry brown animal with a human face. It huddled on the cave floor, rocking back and forth, its lower lip quivering.

"Why did you do that?" it howled. "That hurt!"

Angus stared speechlessly at the creature.

"You should apologize!" insisted the animal. It waited for a moment and when no response came from the dumbstruck Angus, it yelled, "APOLOGIZE!"

"Ivy?" Angus asked tentatively. "Is that you?"

The animal's eyes glistened with tears. It brushed them away quickly and glared at him. "Apologize."

"I'm really sorry. I didn't realize it was you. You startled me. But what kind of animal are you?" asked Angus.

The creature stood. It appeared to be a biped. It balanced well on two legs and its head was level with his waist. It gripped his hand with its paw and began skipping while dragging him toward the opening of the cave.

"We've got to hurry back," it said. "Granny will be really mad if she knows we're here."

"Who's Granny?" said Angus. "Ivy, where are we?"

"You're silly!" giggled the little animal. "Where did you leave your skin? It's really snowing now."

"My skin?" asked Angus. "What are you talking about?"

"Your skin. It's a long way back to the village. Did you leave it on the floor?" The furry creature let go of his hand and scurried along the cave wall. Not finding whatever it was searching for, it looked questioningly at him. "You didn't leave it outside, did you?"

"Gus! Bonnie! Where are you? It's not safe up here! Come here this instant!" Angus heard a female voice calling from outside the cave.

The animal gasped, covering its mouth with a paw. It looked at him with horror-stricken eyes. "Oh no! It's Granny!"

"GU-US! BON-NIE! GU-US! BON-NIE!"

"Maybe we can sneak past her. Get back before she does. Pretend we were never here!" whispered the frantic animal.

Angus had no idea who Granny was, why Ivy was so scared of her, or where they were supposed to get back to. But it occurred to him now that the moss was not insulating his clothing as well as he would have hoped, and wherever Ivy proposed they should go would probably be warmer than this cave. And if not, he could always refer back to survival option number four and wear her like a coat.

"Okay," he agreed simply.

The furry, two-legged creature scrambled out of the cave opening. Angus crawled out behind her and climbed over the boulder. The wind whipped hard pellets of snow at his face and body. He had half a mind to climb back into the cave and hunker down until the blizzard ended but now he couldn't see Ivy.

"Ivy!" he yelled. "Where did you go?" He stumbled away from the rocks and launched his body into the blowing snow. He was going to die from exposure. This was a stupid plan.

Rethinking his strategy, he turned back toward the cave, but he couldn't see two inches in front of his face. He was thoroughly disoriented in the whiteout.

Angus realized his situation was disastrous and growing worse. He needed to figure a way out of this mess. Of course! The World Jumper! He didn't have to freeze here in this strange world. He could pull the trigger on his rewired scanner and jump to a warmer world. Ivy would find him again. He reached into the waistband of his jeans and pulled out ...

... a handful of moss.

Where was the World Jumper?

A hairy paw gripped his arm. "There you are, Gus! What were you thinking? You could have been killed!"

Angus spun around and looked directly into brown eyes framed by wrinkles and frowning gray eyebrows. Pursed pink lips chastised him.

"And where is your skin?" The voice was familiar.

Angus gazed at the fur-covered animal, which bore an uncanny resemblance to the new Ivy. He thought it was probably the same species. He noticed a bow across the animal's back and a quarrel of arrows tethered around the animal's waist. Except that animals don't carry weapons. And then Angus realized this was no animal.

"Granny?" he asked incredulously. What was his grandmother doing here in the snow?

"What is wrong with you, boy? The cold must have affected your brain!" Granny considered him for a moment. She unwrapped a fur from her body and wound it around his shoulders. "Now quickly, I've left Bonnie in the trees. We need to get out of here before the monster returns."

Monster? What monster? What kind of world had he jumped into?

Angus grabbed the back of Granny's fur so he didn't lose her in the blizzard. He stumbled along behind her.

"What's gotten into your head!" she continued scolding as she trudged through the snow. "How many times have we told you to avoid this area? Don't hunt on the plateau. Every morning we tell you the same thing. One of these days the monster will be here waiting for you!"

His grandmother plodded onward undeterred by the buffeting wind. Angus could see nothing except for the back of the fur garment to which he was clinging. If he lost his grip, he would lose her. How did she know where she was going? It was like she had an internal global positioning system. Snippets of her tirade gusted past his frozen ears.

"... follows you everywhere! ... endanger both your fool lives! ... your sister! ... be responsible! ... copies everything you do! ... her safety ... ."

Sister? Whose sister? What was his grandmother talking about?

Angus focused on his grandmother's back and kept walking. He bumped into her when she stopped suddenly. He looked past her and realized they were standing in the grove of trees he had encountered earlier.

"Gus! Gussy!" he heard and then grunted when a small furry body flung itself at him. An adoring face gazed up at him.

"Ivy?" asked Angus. He gently touched the face of the small human and pushed back the fur that rimmed her head. Loose light waves of fine brown hair clung to the small skull. The little girl's blue-green eyes sparkled and Angus realized with a shock that they looked just like his.

"You're not Ivy," he whispered under his breath.

"Come on now, you two. We have to get back to the village before dark. Your mother will be worried," ordered his grandmother. She turned back and looked at the children. "Bonnie! Put your hood on! It's bad enough that Gus lost his skin. I don't need both of you catching your death out here!"

The girl grabbed her hood and pulled it back over her head. She tipped her head down as she tucked her hair inside.

"Ooh! Pretty!" she pointed at Angus's purple rhinestone-encrusted sneakers. Granny looked in the direction Bonnie had pointed and squinted.

"What is it?" she asked. She wandered closer and peered down at Angus's feet. She shook her head and looked at Angus. "My eyesight's not what it used to be, but just what are you wearing on your feet?"

Angus looked at Granny's feet and then at Bonnie's. Their legs and feet were encased in thick fur skins and wrapped with leather bindings. Angus felt a pang of envy as he took in his own cold, wet, purple canvas feet.

"Sneakers," he answered.

"Sneakers," repeated Bonnie dreamily as she reached out to stroke them.

"Sneakers," snorted Granny. "Well, you'd better thank your lucky stars if you don't have frostbite by the time we get back to the village. Come on then!"

She set off down the hill with purpose. Bonnie smiled at Angus, grabbed his hand, and they followed their grandmother.

3

The Village

Angus dropped Bonnie's hand to wrap the fur more tightly around his chest. He shivered and walked faster. He wasn't sure how far the village was but he hoped there would be a roaring fire where he could warm himself.

He remembered the last time he'd felt this cold. He'd been forced to walk the plank off a pirate ship called the Fearsome Flea splat into the middle of the Puget Sound. The water had been icy cold and he might have succumbed to hypothermia if he hadn't been rescued by Ivy who'd taken on the form of an orca.

He had been marooned on an island with a pirate captain named Hank who had lit a bonfire and baked cookies to warm him up. Together they had built a boat and reclaimed the Fearsome Flea.

That had been his first excursion to a parallel world, a world existing in the same time but another version of reality. For example in the pirate world his respectable math teacher was a nasty, mean-spirited pirate. And his alter ego, the other version of himself who had disappeared when Angus had arrived, stuffed cannons for a living.

It had taken Angus a while to figure out just how his invention, the World Jumper, had sent him to the pirate world. He'd learned that a combination of baking soda and moisture energized the device. And then he accidentally triggered the World Jumper again and sent himself … .

Where was he exactly? This world was covered in snow and ice. In this world his grandmother wore animal furs and carried a bow and arrow. In this world he had a sister.

"Mommy is going to be mad, Gussy," said Bonnie blinking up at him. She chewed her lip. "You're going to be in trouble."

Angus's teeth chattered. He stomped his feet to get blood moving in them.

"He's already in trouble," muttered Granny. "With me."

"Squirrel!" hissed Bonnie.

"Where?" Granny spun around.

Bonnie silently pointed at the midsection of a large cedar tree. Angus's mouth gaped open when he saw the animal clinging to the trunk of the tree. In shape and color it did resemble a squirrel. But this arboreal creature was the size of a large tom cat. It was enormous!

Granny unstrapped her bow, strung a bone-tipped arrow, aimed at the squirrel, released the arrow, and missed.

Granny shouted, "Duck!"

The squirrel raced off, the arrow shot straight up in the air, and Bonnie tackled Angus to the ground. The arrow whizzed down to the ground and sliced into the snow mere inches from Angus's ear.

Bonnie climbed giggling from Angus's back. Angus spat snow from his mouth. Granny kicked the trunk of the tree with a fur-wrapped foot before yanking the arrow angrily from the snow. She pointed at Bonnie. "Don't you tell your mother!"

Granny stomped off. Angus sat in the snow staring after her.

"She hasn't been able to hit anything in a long time," sighed Bonnie. "She can't see." Then a hint of a smile tugged at her lips and she giggled.

"So she can't see. What's so funny about that?"

Bonnie shook her head. "Not that. That." She pointed at the packed snow. A perfect impression of Angus's face was squished into the white powder.

"Yeah. Hilarious." Angus picked snow out of his goggles before climbing to his feet. The two set off after Granny.

The forest floor was steeper now. Granny descended by traversing it side to side. Angus noticed deep notches in the trees around which they walked and turned. The notches must be trail markers. Granny paid the markings no heed and expertly made her way through the forest. For the second time that day he pictured a tiny GPS inside her brain.

The terrain leveled out and low growing shrubs mixed in with the trees. There were gradually more and more bushes and fewer and fewer trees. Bonnie yelled, "Race you!" and ran off past Granny. The small, fur clad girl whished through the deep snow toward what appeared to be civilization.

Angus's amazement grew as he and Granny approached the village. Large curved white posts surrounded the encampment. Smoke drifted over the barrier, probably from the cluster of small huts at the center. He saw brown furry shapes moving throughout the village. Several clutched what looked like spears and marched the perimeter of the camp. He watched Bonnie run to one of them and throw her arms around it. He figured it must be her mom.

As he and Granny approached the gateway through the barrier, an obnoxious stench assaulted Angus's nose. He threw his hand over his face and gagged, "Yuck! What is that smell?"

Granny chuckled. "Don't think you're going to get out of evening chores that easily. It's your turn to muck out the corral."

She nodded her head in the direction of a pen surrounded with the same curved posts as the village's fence. Angus was amazed, elated, and horrified by what he saw. Amazed, because he'd never seen one alive before. Elated, because he had never in a million years believed he'd ever see one. And horrified, because it had probably been ten thousand years since human eyes had seen a ground sloth, let alone a pen full of them.

So if those were giant sloths, to what kind of world had Angus transported himself?

Angus breathed through his mouth and walked closer to the large corral. The sloths looked like overgrown opossums. Several lowed at him like cows and approached the fence. The animals were massive and Angus backed away immediately. The largest one rivaled the elephants Angus had seen at the zoo.

They had five fingers with claws the length of a school ruler. Their fur was the same light brown color of the skins that Granny and Bonnie wore. And the stench coming off of the beasts was unimaginable. It was a wild, oily smell that made Angus's eyes water.

Some sloths grazed on drying broadleaves piled around the corral. A few smaller sloths napped in stinky piles like overgrown ferrets at the pet store. They appeared to be docile and made no attempt to escape the barrier, even though such enormous animals could have pushed through it easily.

"Why don't they break out?" wondered Angus out loud.

"We breed them, of course," answered Granny. "They're no more wild than you or me. The only life they know is alongside humans." She looked askance at him. "Are you feeling alright, Gus? You'd better get home and warmed up."

Angus looked about, wondering which hut was home. He was embraced by a tall furry woman who kissed the top of his mussed head. Mom?

"What is this?" she asked tugging on his safety goggles. She wondered at his clothing. "What are you wearing and where is your coat?" He blinked at her and began to answer, but she interrupted. "That was a stupid thing you did! You are lucky you weren't eaten! And Bonnie up there with you! How many times have I told you not to go up there?" She squeezed him tighter. "Let's hurry home and warm you up."

She wrapped her arm around his shoulder and herded him to the door of one of the many large wigwam structures that populated the village. The posts that surrounded the village were also the framework of the dwellings. The round, white posts were thick at the bottom, curved like a crescent, and tapered to a point. Large furs were wrapped and tied around the posts.

His mother's alter ego pushed aside a heavy fur drape and entered the hut. Angus followed and pulled the drape closed behind him.

The inside of the circular hut was deceptively large. Small torches at the entrance to the round room cast a dim yet cozy light on its interior. In the center of the room a peat fire burned, its smoke escaping through a small hole in the ceiling. To the left of the door, long woven sheets hung from the domed ceiling and divided the hut into two small rooms and one large central area. Angus could see bedrolls and blankets piled in the small rooms. Those must be the bedrooms.

Angus saw some interesting tools directly across from the door. One of them was a large wooden wheel resting on a wooden base. A clump of fur rested on a spearhead and yarn dangled from the wheel. He thought it might be a spinning wheel. Alongside it was a medium-sized frame of wooden posts and struts. Yarn stretched across the frame from one end and turned into fabric at the other end. Was that a loom?

To the right of the door, a short table held the makings of a meal. A sharp utensil that resembled a knife rested beside a pile of greens, a chunk of smoked meat, and a clay jug of liquid. Bonnie sat curled on a pile of furs near the fire, sipping something from a cup. No longer wrapped in her coat, she was a thin, small child of maybe five or six. Her wavy light brown hair was mussed, her cheeks were rosy, and from the way she was attacking that cup, she was ravenous.

The woman who looked like Mom pushed a stack of knitted garments at him. "Get out of those wet things." She crouched at the fire and poked at a large carved bowl resting among a circle of stones. "Soup's been warming all day. I'll dish you up a bowl."

He knew she wasn't technically his mother. She was his alter ego Gus's mother, but she looked and sounded just like Mom, she hurried and scurried just like Mom, she fussed and fretted just like Mom. He hadn't realized how much he'd missed his own mother until he saw her alter ego stirring soup.

Angus untied and kicked off his wet sneakers. More cold than shy, Angus turned his back and eagerly stripped off his clothes. Piles of moss cascaded out of his pants and shirt. He brushed a few clinging strands from his legs and chest. He unfolded the garments Mom, no, his mom's alter, maybe he'd call her Mother, had given him.

First, he put on a light, long-sleeved woven shirt in a light brown color. He pulled it over his head. It was light but amazingly warm. The pants were made from the same material and fitted like the undergarments he wore skiing. Next, he slid on a pair of thick, handknit socks. They itched a little but the warmth was welcome. He slipped a heavy cabled brown sweater over his head. It was a bit large and smelled faintly of wet animal.

Last, he looked at the pants Mother had given him. He brushed them with his hand. They were rough suede and felt like a pair of cowboy chaps he'd worn for Halloween one year. They slid easily over the woven long underwear. Instead of a zipper and button, leather laces were strung through small holes in the front of the pants. Angus shrugged and tied the pants closed. He wrapped his toolbelt around his waist, checked to be sure his screwdriver was in its place, and rearranged his safety goggles on the top of his head.

"Hang your wet things on the line and come get a bowl of soup," said Gus's mother.

Angus complied, draping his blue jeans and shirt over the braided leather clothes line strung along the wall. He carefully placed the purple sneakers to the side of the clothes. He wasn't naturally neat: His laboratory at home had its own special organization. But his stint aboard the revolting Fearsome Flea was still fresh in his mind.

He settled down beside Bonnie and eagerly took the reddish-brown cup Gus's mother offered. Both the cup and the serving bowl Gus's mother held looked like no kind of porcelain he'd ever seen. They were matte, slightly rough to the touch, and heavy.

"Interesting cup," he observed.

Gus's mother paused a moment from ladling out a serving and looked curiously at the goggles on top of his head. "Ye-es," she said slowly. "The village elders do a good job making them."

"Do they use some clay indigenous to the area?" asked Angus.

Gus's mother stared at him. "Gus, you've helped Granny dig for it. What's that on your head?"

"Something I found," stammered Angus brushing a finger across the goggles.

She shook her head and dipped her ladle into the bowl, pouring the soup into Angus's cup. The ladle was white and appeared to be made from an organic material.

"Is that made from clay, too?"

"Of course not!" snorted Gus's mother. "Your father carved it from bone. You know that."

Angus took it from her hand and examined it carefully. "Cool! Would he teach me how?"

"I suppose you can ask him when he returns from the mammoth hunt."

Angus gasped. "Mammoth?"

Bonnie giggled. "Gus, you're funny today."

"You are acting strangely." Gus's mother placed her hand on his forehead in the time honored tradition of mothers everywhere. "You don't seem to have a fever."

Angus stirred the soup in his bowl while he considered all he'd learned. He was in a world with no electricity. A fire in the middle of a hut was technically central heating, but the family cooked on it also, so it was more like camping. The squirrels were gigantic, the community shared a sloth farm, and his father's alter ego was hunting mammoth. He thought of his own father at home who hunted the occasional rat in the garden shed with a snap trap and peanut butter.

Bonnie's voice interrupted his thoughts. "Can I have that thing on your head?" She grabbed at his goggles.

"No!"

"What about that?" she asked reaching out little fingers to touch his toolbelt.

"Hands off!" he slapped her hand away.

"Gus! Don't strike your sister!"

"You're mean," frowned Bonnie.

"Gus, eat your soup and leave your sister alone. Once you've warmed up you have chores to do."

Angus slurped his soup and glared at Bonnie. She stuck her tongue out at him. He thought Gus must have all the same problems he did, plus one more. Bonnie was licking her bowl clean.

Angus wrapped his hands around the cup and inhaled the aroma of the soup. The steam tickled his nostrils and condensed on his upper lip. He sipped the brown liquid. It was salty and rich and warm and he could feel it making its way down his esophagus into his stomach, heating him as it went. "Ummmm delicious," he breathed.

"Thank you," answered Mother.

"BUUURRP!" said Bonnie.

Angus stared at her and then looked at Gus's mother. She didn't seem to have noticed, so Angus said loudly, "Bonnie, that's really rude. Pretty gross behavior. You should apologize."

Bonnie gaped at him and Gus's mother turned from her work at the fire.

"What is that you're saying, Gus? What should Bonnie apologize for?"

Angus shrugged. "She burped at the table. That's bad manners. She needs to excuse herself."

"What?" Bonnie looked to her mother.

"She burped because she liked my soup. That was the nicest compliment she could give me."

Gus's mother smiled at Bonnie. "Thank you, sweetie." She fixed Angus with a hard stare. "I don't know what's gotten into you today, Gus, but you don't talk to Bonnie like that. Now finish your soup and go do your chores."

Burping was allowed here? That was the most awesome thing he'd heard all day! Angus expelled a loud "BULLLP!" His mother smiled. "Okay, I forgive you, Gus. But the beasts won't clean themselves. Off you go. And don't forget to wear your boots!"

"Boots?" asked Angus.

"Yes, where did you leave them?" asked Gus's mother. Her eyes fell on the purple sneakers resting under the wet clothes. "Where did those come from?" She touched the wet blue jeans and shook her head. "I will never understand where you find half the things you bring home, Gus."

"Aren't they pretty, Mommy?" trilled Bonnie as she fondled the sneakers' rhinestones.

Mother bent down and touched them. "Yes, they are. Very strange. Where did you leave your boots, Gus?"

Angus looked at her blankly. He certainly couldn't tell her that Gus's boots were probably still on Gus's feet wherever in the universe Gus had gone when Angus arrived. He couldn't possibly explain the concept of interdimensional travel, mostly because he didn't totally understand it himself. So he did what came naturally, what he would have done if his own mother had asked him an unanswerable question.

"I don't know," he said.

Gus's mother stared at him and sighed. "Well, I guess you'll have to wear your old boots. And I don't want to hear that they're too tight. I don't have time to make you a new pair right now. Maybe you can ask around the village and see if you can borrow a pair from someone." She tossed some tall fur moccasins at him.

Angus shoved his wool-encased feet into the boots. They were a bit snug but a welcome change from the cold, wet, purple sneakers. He wrapped the leather straps around them and tied them tightly to his leg. He looked at Gus's mother. She was rummaging around the clothesline.

"I suppose you forgot where you left your coat, too?"

Angus gave her a sheepish grin.

She shook her head. "You'll have to wear your good one. I don't like you mucking out the pens with it, but what else are we going to do?" Angus wrapped himself in the fur coat.

"And wear this hat," she ordered, handing him a knit cap. "Now, you'd better get out there or they'll say the Clark family doesn't do their bit to help." She nudged him out the door.

4

Chores

Angus had no idea what he was in for but he knew it was supposed to happen in the sloth corral. He adjusted his goggles over the top of the cap and trudged in that direction. Women and children his age and older walked along the fence line carrying spears. They looked out toward the forest. Most had grave expressions and a few of the children seemed fearful.

Angus continued on his way to the sloths. The stench of the beasts grew stronger. He wondered if he'd ever get used to it, the way you grow accustomed to the smell of your own house but your friends' houses all smell different. He wasn't sure getting used to the smell would be such a good thing.

"There you are!" shouted a fur-wrapped boy standing inside the sloths' enclosure. Angus would know that grin anywhere.

"Hi Billy!" he yelled back.

In Angus's world Billy Roberts was the best friend a guy could have. He was goofy and fun and always eager to join in on whatever game or invention occurred to Angus. Angus had last encountered Billy in the pirate world. That alter ego was a true mayhem-causing pirate. But it had been Billy who'd kept the World Jumper safe.

"I thought you were trying to dodge the doody duty!" laughed the rowdy boy.

"You mean we have to scoop poop?" Angus looked uneasily at the gigantic creatures gathered around Billy. They didn't appear to be aggressive. Angus took a deep breath, grasped the gate with resolve, pushed it open, and entered the corral.

"Here," said Billy handing Angus what looked like a shovel. Leather strips bound a bone scoop to a long staff. Angus took the shovel, pulled the goggles down over his eyes, and began moving the monstrous dung into a pile. If he ever got home, he would never again complain about cleaning the cat box.

"Where do we put it?" he asked.

"In the barrow, of course. Duh!" teased Billy. Angus saw a primitive wooden cart with handles and a misshapen wooden wheel. He scooped the manure into the cart.

When it was full, Billy trundled the wheelbarrow across the pen to a gate on the opposite side. "Are you coming?" he called.

Angus dodged a sloth lumbering toward him and jogged across the pen. He pushed the gate open for Billy who dumped the dray's contents on to a massive steaming pile.

"Ugh!" gagged Angus.

"You do the next load!" announced Billy with a grin.

The two boys took turns shoveling and hauling sloth dung from the corral to the compost heap. After nearly an hour of toil the sun was low in the sky. Angus no longer noticed the revolting nature of the job. His back and shoulders screamed as he lugged the heavy cart for the last time that evening. He parked the wheelbarrow and closed the gate behind him. Billy was refreshing the leaf mounds in the pen from another wheelbarrow while the sloths watched eagerly.

"That's a lot of food to unload," remarked Angus as he hurried over to help.

"I'll be happy when we can take them out grazing again," said Billy. "I hate hauling the food. And there was less dung to shovel when we could let them graze."

"Less poo would be nice," agreed Angus.

"Yeah. Maybe when our dads are back from hunting mammoth they'll kill the monster and we can get the beasts out of this corral. Too bad it showed up right after they left."

Angus mentally listed what he knew so far. All the men were on a hunting trip. The women and children were protecting the village. Everyone was afraid of some dangerous creature that ate gigantic ground sloths.

Angus didn't even want to contemplate how large a predator that would be. "Have you seen it?" asked Angus.

Billy stared at him. "What are you asking me that for? I was with you the first time it attacked, don't you remember? We started locking the gates and posting sentries the next day."

"Yeah. Right," said Angus. He couldn't ask what the so-called monster looked like if he'd supposedly already seen it. He threw the last load of leaves to the sloths and wiped his hands on his leather pants.

"Speaking of sentries, would you take my shift tonight? I'm too tired. I'll take your shift in the corral in the morning. Deal?" said Billy.

"Sure," Angus said. He didn't know what he'd have to do on sentry duty, but he was eager to get away from the stinky animals for a day.

"You tell Granny, okay?" said Billy.

"Granny?" asked Angus. "You mean my grandmother?"

"Of course. She is the captain of the sentry after all."

His grandmother the "captain of the sentry"? Angus left Billy and went searching for her. He didn't have far to go. She was at the village entrance. A group of tough-looking boys clutching spears loitered around her. She appeared to be leading a meeting.

As he approached, he heard her say, "It's been nearly a week since the monster took one of our beasts. Expect an attack tonight. I want three of you in the corral. Two on this gate. Five of you sweep the perimeter. It will be a dark night with the waning moon, but when you see the crescent at its highest point, second shift begins. I hear about anyone sleeping when you're supposed to be patrolling, you get dung duty for a week. Understood?"

The boys grumbled in assent.

"Good," she barked. "First shift let's have Jack, Paul, and Melvin at the corral." Angus heard a groan. "What Melvin, you want first *and* second shift?" Granny threatened the tall, gangly boy who had complained.

"No ma'am," his voice cracked.

"That's what I thought," she replied. "First shift I want Ralph and Billy on the entrance." Her eyes scanned the boys' faces. "Where is Billy? Gus, what are you doing here? You're not on sentry tonight."

"I'm filling in for Billy," said Angus.

"Why, that lazy—" began Granny. She sighed. "Okay, then. You're on the entrance with Ralph. First shifters choose your second shift replacements and get to it."

Angus watched the other boys tap each other on the shoulder. He noticed one of them was watching him keenly. The boy caught his eye and said, "Swap you."

Angus nodded in agreement and watched the sentries disperse. Only Angus, Granny, and a short, solidly built boy remained by the gate.

"Gus, Ralph." Granny addressed them gravely. "The monster is sure to strike tonight. It's been five days since its last attack. I'm expecting it to head directly for the corral, which is why I've posted three sentries there. We don't know much about this creature though so stay alert." She blinked at Angus. "Gus, where is your weapon?"

"I ... I," Angus stammered.

"You'll have to get it after you and Ralph have barred the entrance. Now hurry. Night is almost here," huffed Granny. "I need to speak with the boys in the corral." She bustled off.

The gates of the entrance were constructed of the large curved posts that encircled the village. They were much larger versions of the gates in the sloth corral. Ralph began untethering the first gate. He looked over his shoulder at Angus. "Are you just going to stand there and watch?"

Angus hurried to the other gate and struggled to unknot the braided leather binding. He loosened and removed the tether and the gate shuddered and swung shut. The other gate slammed into it and Ralph began tying the two gates together with the leather rope. Angus followed Ralph's example and together they secured the entrance.

"I hope no one needs to enter or leave anytime soon," said Angus.

Ralph stared at him. "No one would dare be outside the gates after sundown." He turned toward the gate and peered outward into the dark. "Get your weapon," he ordered.

Angus tried to imagine what Ralph was watching for. He had a feeling he'd know it when he saw it. And he knew for certain that he didn't want to see it. An icy shiver crept down his spine and he hurried off to the hut to look for a spear.

Angus could tell from the worried look on her face that Gus's mother was not pleased to hear he had taken on Billy's shift. She said nothing but handed him a pair of fur mittens. "It's bound to get colder tonight," she said. "Take my spear. It's longer and sturdier than yours."

Angus grabbed the larger of the two spears and pecked Gus's mother on the cheek. She forced a wavering smile and Angus stepped into the darkness.

If he hadn't been anxious about the "monster" before, the reaction of Gus's mother would have given him reason to worry. Paleontology was not his area of expertise; he would much rather visit aeronautical and science museums than natural history museums. And honestly, the only prehistoric animals he'd been even remotely interested in were the dinosaurs. And that was when he was Bonnie's age.

He vaguely recalled that megafauna like ground sloths and mammoths lived in the Pleistocene Era. What predators were alive then? And would those same predators exist in this world?

He figured Ivy would know the answers to those questions. But she wasn't here. Angus feared he'd never see his friend again. Even though he had a mother, sister, grandmother, and a father in this world, he suddenly felt very, very alone. Ivy was the only person who truly understood Angus. She had also lost her connection to home. She was also traveling through strange worlds. She always knew what he was talking about without him having to explain everything. The loss of his best friend weighed heavily on him.

As he thought about Ivy he ceased to think about his surroundings. For a moment he forgot where he was and what he was supposed to be doing. He was brought to his senses by the sight of a shadowy figure approaching him quickly. At first he thought it was Ralph but as the figure drew closer, Angus realized it was walking on four legs, not two. The figure was large, indistinct in the gloom, and the size of a small pony.

Angus clenched the spear with white fists. He jabbed it ineffectually in the space in front of his body. "Get!" he said shakily. He tried to yell but his voice had frozen in fear.

The creature was upon him, huge and looming. It reared back on its hind legs and landed its front paws heavily on his chest. Angus was knocked to the ground and the hot, meaty breath of the largest dog he'd ever seen was in his face. He saw drips of saliva on enormous pointed teeth and a tiny gasp escaped from his closed up throat.

5

Gus Stops Traffic

"Hey, kid. It's a little early for Halloween, isn't it?"

Gus stared at the group of teens laughing at him. Where did they come from? Were they back from the mammoth hunt already?

They didn't look like any of the village teens he knew. They wore strange clothing. Colorful undershirts covered with symbols he'd never seen before. Woven blue pants, some with holes in the knees. Colorful shoes. No hats or furs. He looked at his own attire. Thick fur boots, heavy sloth fur coat, squirrel hood. He was feeling a bit warm. He propped his spear against the bench he was sitting on and pulled off his mittens.

One of the older boys shook his head and rolled his eyes. "Weirdo," he said.

Gus watched the teens walk past and closed his eyes. His head hurt. Granny was forever scolding him, warning him not to go to the plateau, telling him one day he would be all alone in a snowstorm and freeze to death. Maybe today was that day.

Last winter he had gotten so sick. He'd had such a high fever, but then he had felt like he would never be warm again. Mother and Granny had taken turns sitting up with him, wrapping him in cold compresses, feeding him mammoth broth drop by drop, or at least that was what they'd told him when he was conscious again.

He didn't remember the being sick. But he did remember the dreams. They had been strange hallucinations of flying sloths and mammoths with his father's head. They had been funny and sometimes frightening, and they had been so real. Only when he was feeling better and had woken from the thick slumber of the deathly illness did he realize the bizarre occurrences had been fever dreams.

Was he hallucinating again? Were these fever dreams?

He opened his eyes and looked around. There was a giant slab of flat, hard rock under his feet. It stretched from side to side as far as he could see. Straight ahead was a large body of water. He could see several vessels floating on it in the distance, and many more tied to a wooden platform stretching over the water.

He was resting on a bench. It was built far better than anything he'd ever seen in the village. The seat was made of thin strips of identically sized wood. The arm rests were crafted of a hard shiny material he'd never before seen. It made a loud *twang* when he tapped it with the bone tip of his spear.

If he was unconscious and dying in the snow, at least he was having a fantastic dream.

He took his spear and headed off down the flat stone path. Villagers he didn't recognize bustled past. He was surrounded by strangers. He had never seen so many people in one place, not even on feast days. The colors of their clothing screamed at him. None of them wore the furs and brown woven sweaters he was used to seeing. Large stone and wood buildings towered above him. Sometimes they blocked the sky.

He walked along the path, head tilted back, searching for the sun. A mastodon scream blared directly in front of him. He covered his ears in shock and strong hands pulled him back. Something very fast, shiny, and colorful sped past him. He gasped for breath.

"That was close! Didn't you see the red light?"

He looked into the concerned face of a woman about his mother's age. She was pointing into the sky at a strange rectangular object swinging above a wider hard black path. The object was long and green with three large circles inside. One of them glowed a bright red. As he watched, another of the circles began to glow a bright green. The woman and several other adults ventured across the black path. He joined them.

Shiny, colorful, humming animals surrounded the path. They differed in shape, size, and color, although the majority of them were shiny gray or dirty white. He could see through their fronts. Some animals held one human, some held several. He reached out a hand and touched one of them. It felt hot and growled at him. He pulled his hand back quickly.

He turned in a slow circle, amazed by what he saw. The animals had eaten the humans, but the humans were still alive inside them. As he stood staring, one of them blared, and then another. Soon they were all bellowing at him. He dropped to his knees, hands held tightly over his ears, and hoped he wouldn't die in the stampede.

"Dude, what are you doing?" A hand on his arm pulled him to his feet. It was his good friend, Billy. "You can't hang around in the middle of the street! The light just changed. Come on!"

His friend tugged him through the herd of shining animals and to the foot path on the other side. As soon as the boys were out of the way, the animals began moving. Several humans waved fists and fingers at him from the bellies of their beasts. One shouted, "Didn't your parents tell you not to play in traffic?"

Gus shook his arm to free it from Billy's hand, which was still clamped tightly around it. Billy released his grip and said, "Are you feeling okay, dude? You don't look so good. I mean, what is that you're wearing?"

Gus looked at Billy's clothing. He was dressed like the group of teens. He wore woven blue pants in a shorter length that stopped just above the knee. Strange black shoes that came up to his ankle. A black shirt with symbols stuck to it. Gus touched the shirt with a finger.

"Yeah, awesome, isn't it? My dad let me have it. It's one of his old AC/DC tour shirts. It's a little big. Some work with the weights and it should be cool though." Billy flexed his biceps and puffed up his chest. "Aren't you hot?"

"Yes, but I'm dying. And hallucinating. That's what happens when you freeze to death."

Billy looked at him strangely. "What the heck? Dude, there's water pouring down your face. It's like you're practically melting in there."

"They'll find my body frozen on the plateau. If the monster doesn't eat it first."

"Dude, you are totally morbid today. Where'd you get that cool spear? Can I try it?"

Gus handed Billy his weapon before fainting on the sidewalk.

6

Together Again

Angus lay beneath the panting animal, the spear knocked from his hand and just out of reach. Drool oozed from the slavering beast's gaping mouth. The weight of the canine crushed Angus's chest making it difficult to breathe. Warm air drifted from the giant hound's long gray muzzle.

Should Angus fight with all his might against the vicious creature? Or should he lie still and play dead? As his feverish mind ran rapidly through scenarios, the dog's tongue began licking his face up and down.

"Yuck!" gagged Angus as his voice suddenly returned. He shoved the animal off him. The overgrown canine jumped around, wagging its tail enthusiastically. "Get off me, you dumb dog!"

"Hey, who you calling a dog? Have you ever seen a dog this big? Look at me! I'm huge!" announced the gleeful animal. "I'm a dire wolf! *Canus dirus.* Grrrrr!" The wolf grinned sharp glistening teeth at him.

"Ivy!" shouted Angus and threw his arms around the neck of the mangy beast. He inhaled the wet, musty stench of her thick gray fur. The wolf whined happily.

"I thought I'd never see you again," said Angus stepping back to better observe her current manifestation. "Wow! You're not kidding. You are huge!"

The dire wolf was about five feet long and was considerably larger than any gray wolf he'd ever seen at the zoo or that time Mom took him to the wolf sanctuary. Its legs were stocky and sturdy and its teeth were abnormally large.

"Gus! Who you talking to over there?" called Ralph.

Angus looked quickly at Ivy. He had a feeling Ralph wouldn't understand this. "One of the guys," Angus yelled into the darkness.

"Well, talk later! We need two sets of eyes over here!" complained Ralph.

"Be right there," Angus shouted back. He whispered to Ivy, "Don't let any humans see you. They're heavily armed and I don't think they'll appreciate having a dire wolf in their village. How did you get in here anyway?"

"I dug under the fence."

"I'm on duty until midnight or whatever time it is when the moon is at its highest point. Find me then when I'm by myself. Can you keep out of sight until then?"

"Not a problem," whispered Ivy slinking away. Within seconds her gray fur blended into the night.

Angus hurried to the village entrance and took his place beside Ralph who was staring anxiously into the black distance.

Angus leaned wearily against the perimeter fence just after midnight. His eyes ached from staring at nothing for hours when he should have been curled up warmly asleep. Ralph had spent the time gasping and pointing at nothing. When he'd tired of that, he'd taken to poking Angus in the ribs and grunting, "Are you still awake? You haven't fallen asleep, have you?"

Angus wondered whether pairing him with Ralph was Granny's way of punishing him for being on the forbidden plateau with Bonnie.

Sometime in the late evening, Mom had arrived with a bowl of steaming soup. He had offered to share it with Ralph. Ralph had insisted they take turns eating so they wouldn't be distracted from the watch. Naturally, Ralph had said, he should eat first since he'd technically been at his post longer while Angus had gone to locate his spear.

By the time Angus got around to trying the soup he was so hungry and tired that he barely noticed the chunks of lard floating on its cold surface. Now he understood why Billy had been so eager to take an extra shift in the sloth pen. As bad as it was to shovel endless amounts of reeking, gigantic poop, working alongside Ralph was a far worse job.

Angus felt a gentle nudge below his shoulder. He spun around and saw two eyes shining in the dark. He instinctively clutched his spear.

"Ivy?" he whispered. She whined at him in greeting. "Wait here a minute. I want to be sure no one is around."

"We're fine," said Ivy. "This nose is incredible. I can smell everything. The nearest guard is clear across the village and one of them has fallen asleep. I can pick up a human's scent long before they ever see me."

Angus shuddered. "I'm glad you're on my side."

Ivy chuckled deep within her grizzled throat.

"How did you find me?" asked Angus.

"Like I said, I can smell everything. I picked up your odor in the forest at the top of the hill and followed it down. I sensed danger so I waited until dark to creep into the village." She licked her chops. "There were two other scents with you in the forest. One of them smelled young and tender."

"Don't even think about it!" said Angus. "That was my little sister!"

"Sister? You have a sister?"

"I know. I was surprised too. But I didn't mean how did you find me in the village. How did you find me in this world?"

"I followed your heat signature," answered the wolf.

"My heat signature?" asked a puzzled Angus.

"Yes! When you jumped worlds you left a trail. I felt warmth and followed it. It led me here," explained Ivy.

"But how did you jump worlds?"

"You know I can find the human version of myself in each world. I always have a sense in the back of my mind of my alter ego's location. Kind of like a homing device," Ivy explained. "My alter ego in the pirate world was on shore not far from the ship. I flew to her, focused all my energy on her, and felt my spirit detach from the seagull body I had been occupying. Then I felt the heat and followed the trail here."

"Fascinating," breathed Angus.

"That was the first time I've been able to control my travel," the wolf said proudly.

"Now, if only I could control my travel with the World Jumper, we could find our way back home," said Angus.

"Well, what are we waiting for? Let's get the World Jumper and see where it takes us next," suggested Ivy.

Angus gazed sheepishly at his fur boots. He kicked at the snow. "What is it?" Ivy growled slowly. "What did you do?"

"I kind of ... misplaced it," mumbled Angus.

"You did WHAT?" snarled Ivy.

"Quiet!" hissed Angus. "Do you want to wake up the entire village?"

"You *misplaced* the World Jumper?" She reared back on her hind legs and sprang on his chest. He was knocked into the perimeter fence.

She opened her gaping maul and Angus wondered how much control his friend Ivy had over this predator's body. The wolf snapped its jaws shut on the safety goggles and wrested them from Angus's head. Ivy settled back on her haunches in the snow and spat the goggles from her mouth.

"You're still in possession of these stupid things but you've lost the most important piece of technology! How did you lose the World Jumper? Where did you lose it?"

"If I knew where I lost it, it wouldn't be lost," answered Angus angrily. He bent over, retrieved his goggles, and wiped the dog drool from them. "Don't you think I'm upset about it too? I don't want to be stranded in this frozen world. It's a lot colder for me than for you." He glared at the dire wolf and defiantly put on the goggles.

Ivy growled deeply in her throat. "So now what's your plan?" She tried to settle her rage.

She had always been prone to vexation and impatience with the mistakes of others, but she was surprised how quickly and strongly this dire wolf body responded to anger. She'd have to get it under control. She knew that the dire wolf had been a formidable predator during the

Pleistocene epoch. It had become extinct about ten thousand years ago along with most other North American megafauna, or huge animals. How was it still alive in this world?

"If we're planning to be in this world for a while, I guess we'd better figure out what this world is," said Ivy.

"There are ground sloths and dire wolves. The humans wear furs and hunt mammoths," said Angus.

"So in this world the large scale extinction of the megafauna didn't happen," Ivy said.

"What does that mean?" asked Angus.

"Well, you know that scientists disagree about what caused the extinctions. Some think the species of large animals died because of severe climatic changes. They simply starved to death," said Ivy.

"I thought the impact of an asteroid killed them," said Angus.

"An asteroid impacting the earth would have caused changes in the climate, like I said," said Ivy.

Angus rolled his eyes.

"Then there are the theories of disease spreading among the animals," added Ivy.

"What about over hunting by humans," said Angus.

"Yeah, that's one," said Ivy.

Angus looked at the dire wolf. "Clearly none of those things has happened here. So we're in a world in which modern humans and ancient animals coexist." He thought about this for a moment. "Or kill each other."

"Hunt or be hunted." The massive wolf curled back its lips and bared its teeth in a grin.

Their conversation was interrupted by a booming horn in the direction of the sloth corral. Angus heard shouts and saw torches appearing at the entrances to huts around the village.

"Ivy, you'd better hide," began Angus, but the dire wolf had already disappeared.

7

A False Alarm

Angus grabbed his spear and raced toward the village entrance. He passed the Clark hut and saw Bonnie peering out from the doorway. He shouted, "Stay inside!" and rushed toward the sloth corral. Granny stood on an elevated platform, her white hair whipping about her head, barking orders to the women and older children as they appeared with their spears and torches.

Angus spotted Billy at the edge of the crowd and jogged toward him. "What's going on?"

Billy glanced at him quickly and then turned his head back toward Granny. "The sentries noticed a large hole under the fence. They think the monster dug into the village! Granny is organizing everyone to search the village."

"Where's the hole?" asked Angus.

Billy looked at him. "What difference does it make?"

"Do you know where it is or not?"

"No, but I think Ralph is one of the guys who found it. You can ask him. I'm sure he'll tell you all about it." Billy rolled his eyes. Angus turned to go. "Wait a second," called Billy. "I'm coming too."

It didn't take long to locate Ralph. He was standing in the center of a group of adoring younger boys. He puffed himself up proudly when he saw Angus and Billy approaching. "So, I guess you heard," he announced. "I found a monster hole."

"Yeah, we heard," muttered Billy. He didn't like Ralph any more than Angus did.

"I put myself in harm's way protecting the village," boasted the stocky boy. "Could have been killed, but I had a job to do! I never miss a day's sentry duty, no sir." He looked meaningfully at Billy.

"Whatever, Ralph. Just show us the hole," said Billy.

Ralph shoved some smaller boys out of his way and strutted to the fence. "Right there!" he pointed.

Angus crouched down to examine the large burrow dug beneath the curved fence. The snow was packed down hard so it was impossible to distinguish footprints. Angus had a sneaking suspicion about who had dug this hole. He slid down beneath the fence and scrambled out the other side.

"What are you doing? It's not safe out there!" hollered Ralph.

Billy chuckled to himself and climbed into the hole to follow Angus. "If the monster dug this hole and got into the village, it seems to me it's not safe in there."

Realization dawned slowly on the faces of the boys standing around Ralph. Some of the boys began crying, some ran to their homes, and a few tried to slip into the hole behind Angus and Billy.

"Great job, Billy," said Angus. "What'd you do that for?"

Billy laughed and pointed at Ralph. The boastful sentry stood stiffly at the burrow hole looking uneasily to the left and right. "I couldn't help it. Look at him."

Angus coaxed the frightened boys back into the village and then turned to look at the pile of snow where an animal had cast the diggings. He peered at the ground looking for impressions in the snow. He wanted to turn on his penlight but didn't feel like explaining electricity to Billy. He waited until his eyes had adjusted to the gloom. The faint shadows of indentations were just about the size of a large muzzle sniffing along the fence searching for a family member, a loved one, a lost pack mate. This was obviously the hole Ivy had dug when she was looking for him.

"Let's get back inside," he called to Billy. "Whatever made that hole, it wasn't a monster."

The two boys crawled into the hole backwards, scraping the pile of snow with them as they went. They attempted to patch the hole, but as anyone who's ever tried to refill a hole knows, there's always less to go back in than you took out in the first place.

"There is no monster in here," Angus declared to Ralph. A look of relief passed over the jittery sentry's face but was quickly replaced with a scowl.

"Of course there is!" He crossed his arms on his broad chest and swaggered. "The hole is right there! You saw it yourself!"

"Oh yes," agreed Angus. "Some sort of animal was in here. No doubt about that. It might even have been the monster. But the tracks outside the fence go in two directions. Something came in, but something also went back out."

Ralph gaped at him. Apparently it had never occurred to him to check for paw prints.

Billy stared at Angus but said to Ralph, "Guess you should have investigated before you sounded the alarm. You'd better tell Granny to call off the search. I wouldn't want to be you right now. Let's go warm up, Gus." He put his arm behind Angus's back and hustled him away from Ralph.

As soon as they were out of the sentry's earshot, Billy seized Angus's arm and whispered,

"I was out there with you. I know you're not telling the truth. Those tracks only went one way—inside! What's going on?"

"Let's just say I know what, or rather who, those tracks belong to and I don't want Granny and Ralph and a bunch of spear-wielding moms to find her," Angus replied. "She's not dangerous."

Billy blinked at him. "Who's not dangerous?"

"Ivy. Trust me on this, okay?"

Billy regarded him seriously, then quirked a smile. "Of course! Especially if it means I can go back to bed instead of staying up all night in the freezing cold searching for a monster. I'll see you later."

Angus waved goodbye to Billy and hurried off home. As he approached the hut, he saw a large gray dire wolf lying in front of the door, head resting between its paws. Ivy lifted her head and sniffed the air. She thumped her tail in greeting.

"Ivy! You should be hiding," said Angus hurrying to her side.

She stretched her mouth wide in a huge yawn and raised her massive hind quarters in the air while bowing her head and front half forward. She stood and shook herself awake. "What for? Everyone is by the sloth cage. I thought I'd have a quick nap while I waited for you. What was it?"

"They found your hole by the fence. They're convinced a monster got in."

"A monster?"

"Yeah. They're all running around talking about a monster. Apparently, it's not safe to be outside the village walls after nightfall."

"I wonder what kind of creature this so-called monster is? Pleistocene Era megafauna were huge. It could be lots of things. What predator would hunt at night and have a taste for sloth?" mused Ivy. She lay down in the snow again and began absently licking one of the hut's supports. While Angus watched, the dire wolf began gnawing on it.

"What are you doing?" he asked.

"Hmmm? I haven't eaten all day."

"You're chewing on my house," said Angus.

"I am?" Ivy stopped mid-lick. "It's delicious."

"My house is delicious. That's new," said Angus.

"Well, it tastes like bones."

Angus looked at the hut. He reached out and touched one of the curved posts. It was smooth and hard and tapered to a point at the rooftop. "The architecture is interesting," he began.

Ivy snorted through her long wolf snout. "Architecture. Yeah, right. I call it dinner."

"What do you mean?" asked Angus.

"Your house is built of mammoth bones. Ribs, probably."

"It is?" Angus was astonished and looked more closely at the structure. "It is! That is too cool!"

"And they've wrapped the bones with mammoth fur. It looks like a yurt. You know, those tents the nomads used in Mongolia?" Ivy explained. "It smells fantastic and tastes even better."

"Yeah, well, you can't go around eating people's houses. It's pretty rude."

"The fence around the village is made of bones, too," remarked Ivy.

"I don't recommend you have that for dinner either. Maybe there's something inside you can eat," said Angus.

At that moment the curtain of the hut swung open and Bonnie peered out. The firelight illuminated the snow, Angus, and the enormous dire wolf standing just beyond the doorway. Ivy raised her hackles and snarled. Angus spun around, saw the dinner plate eyes of the little girl, and braced himself for a piercing shriek.

8

The Fever and the Feline

Gus heard the voices before he saw the faces.

"Feel his forehead. He's burning up." Mother's voice.

"Of course he's hot. He's wearing a fur coat." Father's voice.

"Can I have his hat? It's a dead rodent. Too awesome." Billy's voice.

"Look, he's coming around." Mother's voice.

Gus scanned the faces peering down at him. Mother, forehead wrinkled with concern. Billy, grin twisting his mouth. Father. Father!

"Father!" said Gus. "You're back!" He threw his arms around a very surprised Mr. Clark.

"Whoa, easy there. You're cutting off all circulation to my brain." Mr. Clark hugged him back.

"How was the hunt? Can I go with you next time? I'll almost be old enough, and I've been practicing my throwing skills. Where's my spear? I'll show you."

Gus scanned the room he was in. It was unlike any hut he'd ever seen. Light streamed in through clear walls. He could actually see trees and flowers outside through the walls. He was resting on a plush, cushiony pallet raised off the floor. The floor was covered in something resembling fur. Gus wondered what this place was. Was he still dying?

"Yes, young man. I wanted to ask you about that spear. Did you build that in your lab? You know how I feel about weapons," said Mrs. Clark.

Gus looked at Mr. and Mrs. Clark and asked, "Am I dying?"

"Dying?" spluttered Mr. Clark.

"I told you he's ill. He has a fever. I'm putting him to bed," said Mrs. Clark.

Gus wobbled to his feet. "Where's Bonnie?"

"Who's Bonnie?" Mr. Clark asked Billy.

The boy shrugged. "Beats me. I don't know any Bonnies."

"None of the girls at school?"

Billy shook his head in the negative.

"Mother, where is she? Is she still up there? Alone?" Gus grabbed Mrs. Clark's arm.

"Honey, we don't know who you're talking about. Is this 'Bonnie' a new friend?"

Gus stared at her. "Bonnie! My sister! Your daughter! She was with me on the plateau. She's still there!"

Mrs. Clark and Mr. Clark exchanged glances. Mrs. Clark touched Gus's forehead gently, smoothing back his shaggy hair. "Sweetie, I think you're coming down with something. Why don't you head upstairs to your room and rest a while? I'll bring you a nice hot cup of tea."

"Rest? How can I rest knowing Bonnie's all alone, and you don't care? I have to find her!" Gus turned around looking for a way to get out of the very large and confusing hut.

Billy strode to a tall wooden object built into the wall and gripped a shiny ball protruding from it. "Where did you last see Bonnie?" he asked.

"We were in the forest by the plateau. We watched the monster leave its lair. I thought I could hide while it was away, mount a surprise attack when it returned. I was on the plateau when—I don't remember what happened after that. I had a strange dream. Now I'm here in this hut. When did you build this, Father?" Gus sat down suddenly and cradled his head in his hands. His temples were throbbing and he thought he might faint again.

Mrs. Clark sat down beside him and stroked his head. "We need to get you to bed, darling."

"But Bonnie ..."

"I'll find her," said Billy. He walked through the door.

"He fell asleep ranting about this 'Bonnie'," said Mrs. Clark cradling a cup of tea. "His temperature was 103 degrees. Do you know, he wouldn't let me put the thermometer in his ear. Claimed he didn't know what it was. Asked was I going to stick it all the way into his brain."

Mr. Clark chuckled.

"It's not funny! I threatened him I'd stick the baby thermometer in his behind if he didn't cooperate!"

"I'll bet he begged for the ear thermometer!"

"Good thing, too. I don't have a baby thermometer. The medicine should help bring his fever down. You know, I'm worried about him. He's been strange lately."

"I'm telling you, he doesn't have a fever. He was wearing a fur coat and boots in 60 degree weather. Did you see those pants? They were genius!"

"Where ever did he find that costume? I haven't taken him shopping. And that spear? That could have done some serious damage."

"He's a resourceful kid."

"Yes, but this is extreme, even for him." Mrs. Clark sipped her tea. "I'm glad Billy was there and had a cell phone. Imagine!"

"So do you think we've seen the last of his other character? That pirate, what was his name?" asked Mr. Clark.

"Oh, I don't remember. Something vulgar." She put her empty cup in the sink. "He exhausts me."

"Yes. Me, too," agreed Mr. Clark. "But it sure is a great ride, isn't it?"

Sir Schnortle didn't like visitors, especially not that loud, bouncy one who followed his boy around. He had heard the voices and vanished as quickly as his chubby body had allowed into his secret place in the entertainment cabinet. There was a small eye hole in the pine door where a knot had fallen out. His peeping hole was ideally located at a height that allowed him to recline comfortably. He needed only to open one lazy eye to see the entire living room.

The feline had taken a little nap until things calmed down. He awoke to the talking sounds of the man and the woman in the kitchen. He peeked his head out of his hiding space. The room was empty. Making sure not to be seen, he padded softly up the stairs. He listened to the gentle snoring of his boy in the darkened bedroom. He poked his head into the small opening and nudged with his shoulder to open it far enough for his stomach and the rest of his body to squeeze through.

Sir Schnortle inhaled languorously. Ahhhh! The aroma of dead meat. He leapt ungracefully to the foot of the boy's bed and lumbered slowly across his chest. He touched his nose to the boy's. The boy raised a sleeping hand and wiped at a phantom tickle. Sir Schnortle backed away and jumped to the floor. Still not his boy, but at least this one smelled better than that last one.

The source of the enticing scent lay crumpled in the corner of the room. The cat licked his chops, and then grabbed a mouthful of the sloth skin and tugged. He flexed his shoulder muscles and pulled. He stopped, got a better grip, and dragged the skin across the room. He dropped the skin, sat down, and casually gave himself a bath. Then he stood again and pulled it toward the open doorway. Just as he reached his destination, the skin snagged on the doorstop. Sir Schnortle batted at it with his paw. The doorstop twanged and gripped the skin more tightly. The frustrated feline emitted a low hiss, but the doorstop did not respond.

Sir Schnortle sighed. All this exercise had left him in desperate need of a nap. He climbed on to the bunched up fur coat, kneaded it into a comfortable nest, and promptly fell asleep purring.

9

Petting Zoo

"Whoa," breathed the tiny girl.

"It's okay, Bonnie. She's my friend. Look," Angus reached behind to pat Ivy's head but his hand connected with air. He turned, but Ivy had vanished.

Bonnie was gaping. "Why didn't it eat you, Gussy? Mommy says the monsters eat children."

"She won't eat me, Bonnie. She's not a monster. She's my friend. I know it's hard to understand, but no one can know she's here. They would try to kill her. Do you understand? She won't hurt any of us."

Bonnie stared at him with wide eyes. "How can that monster be your friend?"

"She's not a monster. She's a dire wolf. Her name is Ivy." Bonnie was listening intently.

"Wolves are predators; they hunt and kill other animals to survive. Just like us. We're predators, too. And Mother is right, you should be careful around wild animals. They can be dangerous. But this one is different." He paused for a moment and then asked quietly, "Would you like to meet her?"

Bonnie nodded silently.

"I'll see if she'll come back, okay? Ivy, are you still here? Bonnie would like to meet you."

The dire wolf crept out of the shadows. She sniffed the air and sat in the snow a few yards from Angus and Bonnie. Angus said, "Bonnie, this is my friend Ivy. Ivy, this is Bonnie."

"Nice to meet you," said Ivy.

Bonnie gasped. "It can talk! You can talk!"

Ivy lifted a back leg and casually scratched a flea behind her ear. "Of course I can talk. I can also do algebra, conjugate verbs in Latin, and identify medicinal and edible wild plants in the Pacific Northwest. If I had opposable thumbs, I could even knit you a pair of socks." It was too dark for Ivy to see Angus roll his eyes.

"Wow, Gussy! Where did you find it?"

"*Her*," growled Ivy. "Where did you find *her*. And I found him, not the other way around. I sniffed him out." She wriggled her nose in the air. "And now I smell a reason to leave."

The dire wolf clambered to her feet but before she could dash into the shadows, Bonnie had thrown her little arms around the wolf's neck and straddled her like a horse.

"What are you doing!" barked Ivy. "I need to run, and fast! Angus! Get her off me!"

Angus rushed to Ivy's side, but before he could remove Bonnie from the agitated wolf's back, he heard a sound that made his blood freeze.

"Step back slowly, Gus. Bonnie, stay where you are. Don't move a muscle. I don't want to miss."

Angus spun around to see Gus's mother aiming a sharp arrow at Ivy. Ivy cowered and snarled. He shouted, "No!" and threw himself in front of the dire wolf. The arrow released from the bow string, winged harmlessly past Angus, Ivy, and Bonnie, and pierced the side of the hut.

"Gus!" yelled his mother. "What are you doing?"

Angus lay his hand on the dire wolf's head. "This is Ivy, Mother. She won't hurt Bonnie, or me, or you. She won't hurt anyone in this village if you leave her alone."

"I might hurt you if you don't get your hand off my head," Ivy growled softly so the armed adult wouldn't hear.

"Sorry," said Angus. "I was trying to make a point."

Bonnie chimed in, "She's our friend, Mommy. See, look how nice she is." Her mother shouted "No!" but Bonnie bent forward and cuddled Ivy's head. Ivy wagged her tail and whined happily.

"She's a sweet little kid," the dire wolf mumbled to Angus.

"She's a nuisance, if you ask me," Angus muttered back.

Alerted by the loud voices, other armed humans had arrived. Mothers shoved their curious children behind them and stood beside Bonnie's mother, spears and bows at the ready, waiting to unleash their protective fury on the large dire wolf as soon as Bonnie and Angus moved out of the way.

"Everyone stop!" commanded Angus spreading his arms wide. "This is Ivy. She is my friend. She will not harm anyone!"

Ivy trembled beside him, too afraid to attempt escape. Bonnie climbed off her back and stood defensively by Angus. She balled up her tiny fists and took a pugnacious stance, her face scrunched aggressively.

"Dire wolves are blood-thirsty killers!" yelled a rotund woman with a spear tucked under one arm and a squirming boy under the other.

"They're wily pack hunters. Where there's one, there are bound to be more," added a skinny, anxious woman.

Angus muttered to Ivy under his breath, "Did you see any others?"

"I snuck away from them back on the hill. I don't think any of them followed me," answered Ivy softly.

"I hope they don't come looking," he mumbled. To the growing crowd he announced, "It's just her. Just one. She's my pet."

"Pet? What's a pet?" asked Bonnie pronouncing the new word carefully.

"You know, an animal that you live and play with. Like a cat or dog or goldfish. Though a goldfish is pretty boring, if you ask me," explained Angus.

The confusion on Bonnie's face was reflected on every other human face listening to him. "Doesn't anyone here have a pet?" he asked.

"Are the beasts pets?" asked Ralph who had just arrived.

"You, I mean, we, eat the sloths and make clothes from their fur," said Angus. "They aren't pets. They're more like livestock. You don't eat or wear pets," clarified Angus. "You mean to tell me that no one here owns a dog or a cat?"

All the human eyes regarded him blankly.

"What is the matter with your son?" the round woman asked Gus's mother. Gus's mother glared at the woman, an irritating neighbor who had been particularly aggravating lately, and stood defiantly beside Angus and Bonnie in front of the fierce predator who was quaking with fear.

"If Gus says this wolf is a harmless pet, then this wolf is a harmless pet."

"Prove it," challenged the annoying neighbor.

Gus's mother questioned Angus with her eyes. His eyes met hers confidently and he nodded his head. She gulped. "I will prove it to all of you," she declared. She turned to the dire wolf, wrapped her arms around its head, and closed her eyes calmly while the whimpering animal licked her meekly on the chin.

The crowd gasped and Ivy thumped her tail. "Let me try!" cried the plump boy clamped under the neighbor's beefy arm. Another child ran to Ivy before his mother could catch him. He looked uncertainly at the wolf, jabbed her fur quickly, and ran back to the safety of the group. The crowd surged forward, lunging toward the dire wolf.

"Hold on now! One at a time!" ordered Angus. "Get in line!"

If he'd thought the villagers were frightening before when they faced his friend with spears, they were positively terrifying now when they were clamoring to touch her. With Bonnie showing the children how to gently stroke the pet and Gus's mother keeping them in order, one after another of the villagers took turns petting the terrified wolf.

Eventually, everyone in the village had satisfied his curiosity and was convinced that this dire wolf would not eat them. Mothers herded their children back to their huts. Some sentries dutifully returned to their posts while others sneaked off to bed. Gus's mother exhaled loudly and slumped her shoulders.

"Bonnie, to bed," she said wearily. "And you," she pointed at Angus. "Be careful. I still don't trust this mangy, flea-bitten beast, pet or no."

Ivy's ears drooped and she lowered her tail. She looked pleadingly at Angus. "Let me say goodnight to her, Mother," said Angus.

"Make it quick. Dawn will be here soon and you need some rest."

As soon as the heavy curtain of the yurt had closed on Bonnie and Mother, Ivy said, "That was completely humiliating."

"I'm sorry, Ivy. I didn't know what else to do. They would have hunted you down and killed you for sure."

"At least that would have saved me from slow starvation. I still haven't eaten. Maybe I could go chew on one of those stinky sloths."

"I don't think the humans would appreciate my pet stealing their livestock. And I don't think my mom's alter will let me feed you."

"Not likely. After all, I'm just a mangy, flea-bitten beast," snarled Ivy bitterly.

"Sorry, Ivy. She doesn't realize you're really a girl." Angus looked at her sadly.

Ivy raised her snout to the sky and sniffed. "I can't smell anything except human." She loped away.

"Where are you going?" Angus called after her.

"To find some fresh air and breakfast. I'll see you in the morning." The dire wolf was gone.

10

Blood in the Snow

Angus tossed and turned on his pallet in the mammoth yurt. He slept in fits and starts. A mishmash of images he'd experienced over the past week ran through his mind. He saw giant sloths sailing a pirate ship, his father wearing a fur coat and trying to get reception for his cell phone in the crystal cave, and most disturbing of all, sharp spears piercing through Ivy's tiny crow body.

A high pitched caterwaul raised goose bumps along his skin and he woke to an urgent, hushed argument between Granny and Gus's mother.

"I have to go help those boys in the corral."

"You've trained them well. They know what to do."

"They can't face the monster alone. Give me my bow and arrows."

"You can't kill it with an arrow. All you'll do is anger it!"

"Those boys need my help."

"They're probably long gone by now. They know when to fight and when to flee."

"Give me my weapon. I'm going."

"You are not going! What good will it do?"

"You mean, what good will an old woman do, don't you? Say it!"

"Come on, Mom. You know that's not what I mean."

"I know exactly what you mean. I can't hit anything anymore. The quarry is never where I see it. What use is an old, blind huntress?"

Another screech pierced the morning air. A low, guttural moan soon followed.

"Sounds like it's made a kill," Granny sighed. "It's all over now." She slumped down on some furs by the fireside.

Angus heard a series of deep warning barks.

"What's that?" asked Gus's mother.

Angus threw the furs off his body and jumped out of bed. Bonnie, newly awake, blinked at him sleepily. He ran to the door, shoved his feet into boots, and yanked his coat off its hook.

"Where are you going?" demanded Granny.

"Gus, it's not safe out there," said Mother.

"Ivy's out there. I've got to help her!" His words were punctuated by a piercing yowl.

"Who is Ivy?" asked Granny.

"His pet," explained Mother. "The wolf can take care of itself." A loud yelp contradicted her.

Angus grabbed a spear and pushed his way past the women to the outdoors. The noise of a fierce battle echoed through the deserted village streets. The sentries were long gone. Angus stumbled over the loose ties of his boots, paused to wrap them about his ankles, and set off again toward the sloth corral at a run. The low moan of a dying animal ran a bass line under the snarls, barks, hisses, and screams of the monster and the dire wolf.

Angus had nearly reached the pen when he heard a sharp squeal. Adrenaline surged through him and he hurled his body over the gate. The corral was empty. Piles of leaves sat untouched where he and Billy had hauled them the previous evening. Large heaps of fresh dung were scattered over the trampled snow. Where had all the ground sloths gone?

The far side of the mammoth bone enclosure was missing. Angus hurried to it. The uprooted bones lay in the snow outside of the enclosure. They had fallen outward, indicating that they had been pushed from the inside. The sloths must have panicked when they sensed the predator approaching. They knocked down the fence that could have protected them!

Beyond the fence line the snow was stained crimson. Whatever animal had been injured there must have perished. The amount of red snow was evidence that a mega animal had bled to death. He prayed it was not Ivy. A red trail extended from the pool of blood toward the forest. Angus stepped closer and examined it. He could see sizeable tracks in the snow. They faced in the direction of the corral, and the front paw prints had sunk deeper into the snow than the back prints. A large predator must have dragged its kill away from the village. His eyes followed the trail. It stopped abruptly at the carcass of a large sloth pup and the body of an enormous wolf.

"Oh no!" Angus gasped. He tripped over his loose boots and stumbled. He regained his balance and plowed his way through the snow toward Ivy, carefully avoiding the compressed red trail. The dire wolf and the sloth lay side by side, covered in blood.

Angus dropped to his knees beside Ivy. Her tired brown eyes met his anxious blue ones. She lay panting on her side, blood dripping down her face.

"Ivy, are you ... ?" Angus choked back tears and reminded himself that if an animal died while Ivy was in its body, her consciousness would depart the animal and enter another living creature.

"Relax," she panted. "I'm fine. Just a little tired."

"But all the blood!"

"Most of it belongs to that poor sloth. Its throat is ripped open. I took a few hits. The one across my nose really hurt."

Angus examined the dire wolf's muzzle. The soft, fleshy top was slashed open and bled freely. Angus washed it with a handful of snow.

"Ow! Careful, that stings," complained Ivy.

"So this is your pet, is it?" Angus looked up and was startled to see Granny bustling toward him in the early morning light.

"Yes, Granny. This is Ivy."

"Well, Ivy. You've earned your keep. The monster killed one of our beasts but you scared it off before it could make off with the meat. We'll eat well tonight. Gus, why don't you take your pet back to the hut, and get her cleaned up and fed?" She yelled toward the corral where a group of boys stood uncertainly. "What are you bunch waiting for? A personal invitation? Get over here and haul this meat to the village!"

Angus coaxed Ivy to her feet. The canine limped along beside him in the snow. "What was it?" he asked. "What is the monster exactly?"

"It's a lion."

"A lion?" Angus thought for a moment. "You mean a saber-toothed cat? With those long canine teeth?"

"No. I mean a lion. A really, really big lion with some nasty sharp claws."

"Like a lion at the zoo?"

"Similar, but much bigger. I think it might be the *Panthera leo atrox*."

"The panther what?"

"The *Panthera leo atrox*. The American cave lion. In my world their remains were discovered in the La Brea tar pits. Do you have tar pits in your world?"

Angus answered, "Yes. My parents took me there once. I don't remember a lion though."

"You were probably only paying attention to the *Smilodon fatalis*."

"English, please." The dire wolf was beginning to get on his nerves, just like the Ivy in his home world.

"The saber-toothed cat. There were many more of those than American lions found in the tar pits, which suggests that awesome fangs, while looking fierce, didn't make them as smart as the lions." She padded through the snow in silence and then said, "It is confusing though."

Angus waited. She obviously wanted him to ask her, so he did. "What is confusing?"

"In all the studies I've read, the *Panthera leo atrox* preferred open habitats, not forests. The species preyed on North American camels and tapirs."

"There were camels in North America?"

The dire wolf rolled its eyes. "Of course. What do they teach at school in your world? The curious thing is that this lion has chosen a forested area for its territory. And it's prowling around a human village."

"So? The sloths are easy hunting."

"Yes, but remember, I just fought off this lion. A *Panthera leo atrox* is about four times the weight of a *Canis dirus*."

"A can of what?"

"Oh, Angus. Try to keep up. A *Canis dirus* is a dire wolf, remember? What I was saying is the lion should have overpowered me easily. It was strong, true, but I'm still alive with only a few scrapes and bruises. That lion was severely malnourished. There is something wrong with it."

"The sooner we can figure out what that is, the sooner we can rid the village of its threat," said Angus.

11

The Driveway Sentry

Mrs. Clark's eyes shot open. Something had wakened her from a black, deep sleep. She looked at the slumbering form of Mr. Clark lying beside her. In an instant her nocturnal senses were on full alert, honed to precision during the nights of Angus's baby and toddlerhood. Though it had been years since she'd needed to rouse herself from her warm bed to feed him or help him to the toilet, her mothering instincts were a red siren in her brain. Something was wrong. Her baby needed her.

She jumped from her bed and sprinted down the hall to Angus's bedroom. His door was slightly ajar but no soft light drifted through the opening. His nightlight had been extinguished. It was quiet. Too quiet. Her heart was in her throat as she ventured into the room. The shades were drawn tightly over the windows where she'd pulled them that afternoon when her son had fallen asleep. He'd slept straight through dinner. She couldn't bring herself to wake the feverish boy and had tucked him in tightly before going to bed herself a little past ten.

His room was as dark as if she were walking into it with her eyes clamped shut. She felt her way into his bedroom. Her fingers grazed the light switch on the wall. If she turned it on, she might wake him and what if it was nothing? It probably was nothing; she was most certainly overreacting. Anxiety about his strange behavior over the past week was making her act crazy.

She took a careful step. Her foot sank into something soft and fuzzy. She bent slowly and picked up a heavy piece of fur. Angus's costume. She laid it to the side and groped her way to the dresser top. She felt for his nightlight, a tall lava lamp he'd received for a recent birthday present. It had been knocked over and the glass bottle that held the lava material rolled back and forth on the dresser. She flicked the on switch with a finger and placed the glass bottle on to the base. She looked back at Angus's bed. It was empty.

Mrs. Clark exited the room and crept down the stairs. Pale light from the street lamp outside illuminated the hallway and lengthened the shadow she cast as she tiptoed across the floorboards. A settling board creaked when she stepped on it and she winced. No matter. Angus was already awake somewhere in the house, and a marching band parading through the living room wouldn't awaken Mr. Clark.

"Angus," she whispered. "Where are you?"

She peeked into the living room. Perhaps he'd gotten up to use the bathroom and crawled on to the sofa and fallen asleep. A lap blanket lay across the back of the sofa where she'd thrown it before heading to bed. She picked up a pillow off the floor, arranged it on the sofa, and folded the blanket neatly. Nothing out of place.

She looked for Sir Schnortle. He liked to curl up on Mr. Clark's armchair at night. Mr. Clark was always complaining about the tufts of fur he found there in the morning. The chair was empty tonight. Mrs. Clark walked into the kitchen. The sink held signs of one of Mr. Clark's late night snacks, but there were no bread crumbs on the floor, peanut butter smeared on the refrigerator handle, or juice spilled on the floor. In other words, there were no indications that her son had gotten up to make himself a sandwich.

Next, Mrs. Clark checked the bathroom. The door was open, the lights were off, and the towel was dry and neatly hanging where it had been earlier in the day. Angus was not in his bed or on the couch. He had gotten up neither to eat nor to use the facilities. Where was he?

She walked to the hall, the center of the house. She closed her eyes and stood very still. She ratcheted up the level of her supermother powers and listened. The kitchen clock ticked. The refrigerator hummed and the freezer dropped three cubes into the ice tray. The toilet gurgled. Mr. Clark snorted once from the bedroom. A distant vehicle rumbled down the street, squealed its tires, and rumbled away. A muffled Sir Schnortle yowled.

"Sir Schnortle?"

An answering meow came from above. Mrs. Clark jogged up the stairs and called the cat again. Sir Schnortle responded from Angus's bedroom. Mrs. Clark switched on the light and looked around the room. She kneeled on the floor and peered under the bed, and then under the dresser.

"Sir Schnortle? Where are you sweet kitty?"

"Maauuu."

"Are you in the closet? How did you get yourself stuck in there? Silly boy."

Mrs. Clark pushed the sliding door along its track. She raised her eyebrows in surprise when she saw her much-loved and pleasantly plump orange cat lying immobilized on the floor of her son's closet. Part of the reason he could not move was that his front and back legs had been tied together with some sort of leather rope. The fur boot into which his chubby body was stuffed didn't help his situation either.

"Oh! My poor, poor baby! What did the nasty boy do to you?"

She quickly extracted him from the offending footwear and removed the leather ties from his legs. As soon as his front paws were free, she received a sharp scratch for her trouble. Sir Schnortle sprinted out the door. When he was a safe distance away, he turned and glared amber eyes at her.

Mrs. Clark stood and brushed her hand across the angry welt on her forearm. "You don't have to take it out on me! Where is the boy, Sir Schnortle?"

She swatted the light switch on Angus's wall, pulled open the window shades, and gazed vacantly out at the sleeping street. Her eyes focused into narrow slits as they took in the sight of her pajama-clad son pacing back and forth at the end of the driveway, spear in hand.

12

Some Job

The dire wolf sprawled languorously in front of the peat fire. Gus's mother had reluctantly allowed Ivy to enter the hut. Angus thought he had made a convincing case for her acceptance to the family: She had scared away the lion so that no human sentries were harmed and she had prevented meat from being stolen. Good reasons, both, but Bonnie's incessant, "Please Mommy, please, please, please, let us keep Pet! Pleeeeeease!" had probably been the reason Mother had finally thrown her hands in the air and said, "Fine! But you two are responsible for her. I've got enough to do around here."

Ivy looked ridiculous. Bonnie had ransacked her family's homemade medicine supply and doctored all of Ivy's wounds. She had scampered around the dire wolf, bandaging every wound with fine hand-woven strips. Ivy pawed at the wrapping around her muzzle.

"You look like a mummy," said Angus.

Ivy snorted. "Hey, at least I'm warm and my stomach's full." She kept her voice low so Mother didn't hear.

The door banged open. "Gus, we need you. We've got to fix the pen and get the beasts back in before we get another hard snow."

"He was up half the night. Can't one of the other boys take his place?" Mother asked Granny from her seat in front of the loom where she was weaving fabric.

"The entire village was up half the night. We need everyone to help before the beasts are lost. I don't need to tell you what could happen if the men don't bring meat home from the hunt and we have no beasts."

"Okay," Mother nodded. "Gus, go help your grandmother."

Angus put on his outerwear. Ivy lumbered to her feet. "Where's the pet going?" asked Granny hoisting her bow over her shoulder.

Angus and Ivy looked at each other. "With me. She goes with me."

Bonnie grabbed her coat and boots. "Me, too!"

"No, Bonnie. You're too little. You stay with me," said Mother.

"Am not! I wanna go, too! If Pet gets to go, why do I have to stay?"

"You'll get in the way, Bonnie," said Granny.

"You never let me do anything!" yelled Bonnie. "I can help, too! I'm almost as big as Gus!"

Angus and Ivy quickly exited the hut behind Granny as Mother tried to appease Bonnie with offers to use the spinning wheel. They hurried to the corral where teams of boys worked to replace the huge mammoth bones that had been knocked down during the previous night's raid. Ralph and Billy held a vertical rib steady while a lanky dark-haired boy lashed it to the one standing directly beside it.

"Hey, Gus!" yelled Billy, letting go of the bone to wave a cheerful hand at Angus.

"Don't let go!" shouted Ralph. "I can't balance this by myself! Now we've got to start all over again!"

"Where you going?" Billy ignored the complaining boy.

"Not sure," answered Angus. "Granny's got some job for me."

"Here, why don't you take over for me? I've been fixing this pen since the crack of dawn," said Billy.

"That's a lie, and you know it!" whined Ralph. "You just got here."

"We were actually working faster before you got here," said the tall boy to Billy. "Gus would do a better job." This last to Ralph.

"Oh, no you don't. I've got plans for Gus," said Granny. "Maybe you can help him, Ivy." Ivy cocked her head and watched Granny with bright brown eyes. "Back to work, Billy, or you'll have dung duty for the next week!"

Granny hurried through the snow. His real grandmother wore purple velour tracksuits and running sneakers, not sloth fur coats and weapons. She was the leader of a book club, not the leader of the guards. But they were both energetic and agile, real spitfires. Angus ran to keep up with her. She pointed into the forest. "Up there, in the trees. I need you to head up there and bring the sloths back down."

Angus's jaw gaped. "How?"

"The way you always do. Maybe that pet of yours can help." She tightened the quarrel of arrows fastened around her hips and scurried back to the corral, hollering orders as she went.

"Now what?" Angus asked Ivy.

"You heard the lady. Let's go get some sloths." The wolf trotted up the hill into the forest.

13

Carnage in the Kitchen

Mrs. Clark pulled on her bathrobe, brushed her hair, and stepped into her sherbet green slippers. Angus and Mr. Clark looked forward to their weekend pancakes and she was not about to disappoint them. Not even this morning following a middle-of-the-night search for her son.

Angus had been a sleepwalker when he was a young boy. Many times she had opened her eyes in the wee hours of the morning to see him standing motionless in her room. Often, she would awaken to the sound of cereal being poured into a bowl at two in the morning only to find little Angus eating cheerios in his footy pajamas. It had been several years since his last episode of sleep eating.

She had been a bit startled to see him standing outside last night, but that wasn't the first time his nightly excursions had taken him out of doors.

The summer Angus was five, Mrs. Clark had taken him to the local park every afternoon. He had wobbled back and forth on his small two-wheeled bike with the training wheels while she followed behind on the bumpy sidewalk. One day, he had watched a group of older kids race each other through the park on their bicycles. He had immediately insisted his training wheels be removed.

For an hour Mrs. Clark had run behind Angus holding tightly to the seat of his bike, counted to three, and let go. For an hour Angus had balanced for a split second before tipping slowly sideways and tumbling to the ground. To his credit, he hadn't cried, not even when he scraped the heel of his hand the first time or bumped his knee the third time. They had stopped after that first hour, not because Angus had given up, but because Mrs. Clark had twisted her ankle and insisted they try again the next day.

They hadn't needed to try again the next day. Late that night, Mrs. Clark had woken with one of her maternal alerts. When Angus's bed was proven empty and she had searched the entire house for him in vain, a noise from the driveway had caused her to peek out the front door. There he had sat, perched atop the seat of his bicycle, careening up and down the driveway. He had been completely asleep.

So she hadn't been surprised to see him pacing the bottom of the driveway holding that strange, homemade weapon. When she'd attempted to hustle him back into the house, he had protested, insisting that it was his turn on sentry duty. He had told her the monster might come back and asked her again if she knew where Bonnie was. She knew it was a bad idea to wake a sleepwalker and guessed that it was equally unwise to argue with one in the middle of the street, so she had told Angus that the monster had already been killed by a valiant warrior so there was no need for anyone to be on sentry duty and that Bonnie was spending the night with her grandmother. He had accepted this without a word and allowed himself to be led back to bed where he had closed his eyes immediately.

Mrs. Clark had not been so lucky. She had lain awake until just before dawn. She would be asleep still, if she hadn't heard the unmistakable sounds of her son preparing some breakfast in the kitchen. She knew he would begin making the pancakes, and following her sleepless night, she had no energy left to clean up after the eager chef.

Gus stood in front of the sink, hands hidden from view, head bent intently to his task. His grinning face turned to greet her when he heard her footsteps.

"Good morning, Mother! Why don't you relax this morning? I'm cooking breakfast to celebrate the good news!"

"What's that, honey?"

Gus continued to work on something in the sink. "Well, the slaying of the monster, of course! But who did it? Was it one of the men after they returned from the hunt?"

"You remember me saying that?" Angus never had any recollection of his sleepwalking adventures the next morning.

"Of course! Will there be a feast today to celebrate the mammoth kill and the death of the monster?"

"Angus, are you feeling quite well? Has your temperature come down?" Mrs. Clark approached him to lay her hand on his forehead. She glimpsed the sink basin and let out a blood-curdling shriek.

Mr. Clark loved weekend mornings. Sleeping until you were rested. No annoying alarm clocks.

Fragrant coffee with warm, sweet pancakes. Enough time to read as much news as you liked.

Nobody to jostle you awake, yelling "Get up! It's your turn! I've been up all night, and I'm done. You deal with it!" before slamming the bathroom door.

Mr. Clark rubbed his eyes, sat up, and wondered if it was Monday already and he had slept through the weekend. He jiggled the knob on the bathroom door, but it was locked. He put his face to the door jamb and cooed, "Honey, what's going on?"

His delicate, loving wife barked out a collection of syllables that could have made the saltiest sailor reach for his dictionary. He heard the water running in the bath. The unmistakable aroma of Belinda's Bath Salts #45: Nerve Knock-Out drifted under the door. Mr. Clark wondered what his son had done this morning.

He grabbed a sweatshirt and athletic shorts. If he was up this early, at least he could squeeze in a workout. He clomped down the stairs and into the kitchen. His son was working diligently at the sink.

"Good morning, Father!" called the cheerful boy without looking up.

"Good morning!" echoed Mr. Clark. He reached for the coffee pot. It was empty. Mr. Clark sighed and opened the cupboard where the coffee beans were stored. He poured some into the grinder, loaded a fresh filter, and reached for the glass coffee pot.

"Can I squeeze in here, Angus?" He jostled his way to the sink, turned the faucet on, and filled the pot. The hot water had started to drip through the filter into the coffee pot before what he had seen in the sink registered in his brain. He looked into the sink again and gagged. He turned around, drew in two deep breaths, forced the bile in his throat back down, and asked his son, "What are you butchering in the sink?"

"Just a little breakfast, Father. I thought we should celebrate the death of the monster."

"Ummm, yes, Angus. And what exactly is the type of monster you've slaughtered in your mother's kitchen sink?"

The boy laughed. "Very funny, Father. I know these are really small squirrels, but they were all I could find. I set a few snares last night before I went out on sentry duty. That was before Mother told me the monster was slain! Did you kill it, Father? Or was it Billy's father? Or someone else?"

"You set snares in our backyard?" Mr. Clark was equal parts repulsed by the carnage in the kitchen and impressed by his son's hunting skills.

"Of course." Gus dangled three tiny squirrel skins. "They're small, but Mother might have enough to make mittens for Bonnie. When she's back from Granny's." He turned his attention back to the sink.

Mr. Clark looked on, fascinated and disgusted, as his son removed the organs from the furless squirrel carcasses. A flickering light outside caught his eye.

"Angus! There's a fire in your mother's herb garden!"

"Yes, it seemed the best place to roast the squirrels."

Mr. Clark watched his wife's prize rosemary bush burst into flame. His mouth flapped open and shut as the purple flowers of the sage bush popped one after another, distributing sparks freely among the lavender and thyme.

"Water, water!" he babbled before remembering the kitchen fire extinguisher and tripped out the door. Gus wiped his bloody hands on his pajama pants and followed him.

Sir Schnortle jumped to the kitchen counter and looked through the window. Mr. Clark distributed white foam freely around the garden. Gus trampled any herbs that still smoldered after the extinguisher was empty. The cat looked into the sink and his amber eyes glittered. He growled deeply in his throat and licked the saliva that was beginning to flow over his fangs. He thudded into the metal basin and began to eat.

Mr. Clark and Gus re-entered the kitchen. "Okay, I'll call you Gus. Whatever. But you can't go around hunting and cooking rodents in the backyard. Your mother is going to have a fit when she sees what you've done to her herb garden."

"Sorry, Father. I thought she would enjoy someone else making a meal for a change."

"Yes, well, your heart was in the right place. I'll give you that. But maybe stick with eggs next time, okay? Now go take a bath. I'll clean up."

"Thanks, Father." Gus looked confused.

Mr. Clark pointed. "Bathroom, Angus. I mean, Gus."

Gus saw the door and nodded. "Got it."

Mr. Clark turned his attention to the sink. Curled in the basin, hunkered over the squirrels' entrails, licking his chops, sat the fat orange cat. The animal hissed at him, clamped a kidney between his teeth, and clambered out of the sink. He waddled away leaving pink footprints on the tile floor. Mr. Clark watched Mrs. Clark's darling swallow the organ whole before cleaning the blood from his face and paws. Mr. Clark ran, retching, to the bathroom.

14

Snowshoes and Sisters

Angus slogged through the heavy, wet snow. When last he'd been on this hill, he'd been headed in a downward direction. Now that he was bundled in heavy furs and thick snow boots he was fully aware of the steep incline of the hill. It also occurred to him that he wasn't as fit as he'd thought. He huffed and puffed and took more than one break before he'd even reached the first switchback. Ivy loped along ahead of him, her nose an inch deep in the snow, oblivious to the grueling mental and physical effort of her two-legged friend.

She lifted her head, snow thick on her snout, and announced to the air, "I picked up their scent. They should be just around this next bend."

When she got no response, she turned her head and saw the furry brown form of Angus, two switchbacks below. She blew the snow from her muzzle with a deep frustrated exhalation. She opened her mouth to bay at him, remembered the proximity of the sloth, and thought better of it. No need to terrify the dumb animals again and cause a stampede even deeper into the forest.

She trotted down the hill and came upon Angus leaning against a half-dead conifer. "What is taking you so long?" she complained.

"I'm going as fast as I can," panted Angus. "My legs are exhausted from slogging through this deep snow."

"Well, I've got four legs. I should be twice as tired as you."

Angus looked at the dire wolf's feet resting firmly on the snow. His own legs were buried in snow to mid-calf. He remembered the breathless sensation of her knocking him to the ground and sitting on his chest.

"Ivy, how much do you weigh?"

She laid her ears flat against the side of her head and growled. "Didn't anyone ever tell you it's rude to ask a woman her weight?"

"I wasn't asking a woman, I was asking a wolf. And it's not a personal question. It's a scientific one. In all the reading you've done about pleistocene megafauna, what is the average weight of a dire wolf?"

Her ears eased forward. "Oh, well that's different then. If I remember correctly, the average dire wolf weighed anywhere between 110 and 170 pounds. Why do you ask?"

Angus pointed at the wolf's feet. Her toes were splayed across the snow. "I weigh less than that, yet I sink into the snow while you barely disturb it. May I see your front paw?"

Ivy sat in the snow and obligingly raised one foot for Angus's perusal. He examined the pads of her paw in his mittened hand and spread the toes apart. "Of course! It's completely obvious. Why didn't I think of this before?"

"What's obvious?" asked Ivy.

"Your toes spread apart when you walk, creating a larger surface area on the snow. Your weight is spread across a larger area. I weigh less than you, but all my weight is focused into two comparatively smaller spaces. A narrower surface area. If I weigh 80 pounds, each small foot is pushing 40 pounds into the snow. You might weigh 150 pounds, but you have four feet, so that's 37.5 pounds on each foot."

"That's not that big of a difference," said Ivy. "Forty versus thirty-eight?"

"No, it wouldn't be, except for the surface area. The larger surface area your paws give you means you have more snow supporting your body from below the surface. The extra surface area redistributes the weight coming down on the snow from above. The physical structure of your feet helps you to maximize pounds per square inch. In my boots, all my body weight is distributed over a few inches. Your wolf feet spread that body weight over many more inches."

"And?"

"And I need to build myself some snowshoes," finished Angus.

"Angus, we don't have time for that! The sloths are a few switchbacks away."

"Okay, so just a quick fix. I can lash some pine branches to my boots. Won't take but a few minutes. We'll make up the time when I can run across the snow the way you do."

Angus pulled his trusty screwdriver from his toolbelt and stabbed at several low-hanging boughs until he'd ripped them from their respective trees. He overlapped and wove them through each other to increase their strength and rigidity.

"What do you think?" he asked, holding up his handiwork for Ivy's approval.

"They look good to me."

He unwrapped the long leather ties from his boots, wove the straps through the makeshift showshoes, and wrapped the excess around his ankles and up the calves of the boot. The top of the boot flapped open, but the snowshoes stayed fixed to his feet. Angus took a few trial steps on the snow. His feet sank lightly into the powder, but the large pine boughs prevented his feet from being buried deeply.

"Success!" he announced proudly.

"Hey! Did you smell that?" asked Ivy.

Angus's nostrils flared as he drew in a deep breath. "The only thing I can smell is this coat. It's a bit rank."

"Wait here."

Ivy slinked into the forest and Angus was left standing by himself on the narrow trail. With Ivy gone, the forest was still. Angus felt eyes watching him. He turned his head from one side to the other, peering into the dark recesses between the trees. He had an uncanny sensation of fingers creeping along his back, and despite the heavy fur garments a shiver ran through his body. He saw a movement out of the corner of his eye and jerked his head around. Nothing was there. He walked a few steps back down the trail.

"It's nothing. Nothing," he assured himself and turned around.

A soft, hazy morning light filtered through the trees. The air was brisk on his cheeks. The forest felt inhospitable, abandoned, a place to be avoided. He wished Ivy would hurry back. With a thump, snow cascaded off a cluster of salal. Angus glimpsed a dark, crouched form. He didn't wait for the animal to attack. He ran.

"Gus, Gus, Gussseeee! Where are you going?" called Bonnie's voice.

Angus stopped where he stood and let out a loud groan. He slapped his forehead. This was so frustrating! Here was the little kid again, always in the way!

She ran to him and threw her arms around his legs, nearly toppling him over. He grabbed her shoulders and pushed her away.

"Why do you keep following me everywhere? I have important things to do and I can't do them if you're always around."

"I can help you, Gussy!"

"No, you can't. You're just a stupid little kid and you keep getting in my way. Would you get lost!"

Bonnie's face turned red. Tears threatened to spill from her eyes. She gritted her teeth, clenched her fists, and tossed her head.

"You are mean! And you're not Gussy! You don't act like him. You don't even look like him! Not really!" She crossed her arms defiantly across her chest. "Who are you and what have you done with my brother?"

"Nice. You really handled that well, Angus," growled the dire wolf as she stepped over a log and trotted to Bonnie's side.

"Angus! Is that your name? Where's Gus?" demanded Bonnie.

"I'm Gus. Of course I'm Gus. Who else would I be?"

Bonnie glared at him. "Tell her the truth, Angus," said Ivy.

"She won't understand," said Angus. "She's too little. Captain Hank didn't get it, and he was an adult."

"Exactly. Captain Hank was an adult. He'd gotten all serious and lost his imagination, if he ever had one to begin with. Bonnie's a kid. And not just any kid. She's a Clark."

"True," Angus considered this for a moment. "Okay, Bonnie. Here goes. You're right. I'm not your brother. My name is Angus Clark and I'm from another world."

Angus prepared himself to explain the entire story, his World Jumper, the accident, that he suspected he'd changed places with Gus, all of it. But the little girl merely blinked at him and asked, "When is Gus coming home?"

"Soon, really soon," said Angus. "I hope."

"Okay. Neat shoes!" She had already turned her attention to Angus's feet.

Angus looked down. "You mean my snowshoes? Don't you wear them here?"

Bonnie shook her head. "Can I have a turn?"

"No. I'm wearing them. Maybe I'll teach you to make your own."

"And those things on your head? And that belt around your stomach?"

"My safety goggles and toolbelt? Maybe we should start with the snowshoes and see how that goes. But anyway, we have to get the sloths back home."

"I'll help!"

"You're not coming," began Angus.

"You need to go back home," added Ivy.

"Nooooo!" Bonnie wailed.

"Does Mother know you're up here?" asked Angus.

Bonnie scowled at him.

"You'll get into a lot of trouble if I tell her," he said.

"I hope Gus gets back soon. You're a terrible brother." She stuck out her tongue.

He stuck out his tongue at her. The dire wolf raised an eyebrow at him, and he self-consciously pulled the offending body part back into his mouth.

"You need to get back to the village before the adults miss you. We won't tell on you if you go right now," coaxed Ivy.

Bonnie balled her mittened hands into tiny fists and tightened her lips. "Okay," she grudgingly agreed.

"Good girl. Should I go back with you?" asked Ivy.

Bonnie shook her head. "I know the way. He isn't the only one who likes to come up here alone." She darted into the trees like a squirrel and vanished from sight.

15

Herding Sloths

The dire wolf watched Bonnie scamper into the trees and then turned back to Angus. "Let's go get those sloths before it gets any later."

Angus jogged along behind the dire wolf up the hill. Ivy stopped suddenly.

"What is it?" whispered Angus.

"A group of them are around this bend. Can't you smell them?"

Angus wiped his runny nose with a mitten. He shook his head. "No." He sniffed loudly and tried again.

"Ssssh!" hushed Ivy. "You'll frighten them again."

"They aren't afraid of humans. They're domestic sloths, remember? I'm going to walk right over there."

Angus hurried around the bend. Several large heads turned toward him. Lazy eyes regarded him briefly before the sloths turned their attention back to foraging for leaves.

"Come on guys. Let's go back to the village. Here slothy slothy slothy. Here slothy slothy slothy," said Angus lamely as he slapped his knee.

The sloths ignored him. One yawned widely and defecated. Angus walked back around the bend to where Ivy waited, hidden from view.

"Okay. I'm stumped. How do we get them back down the hill?"

"How would I know? I'm a dire wolf, not a sheepdog."

"Ivy, you're a genius!"

"That is true." She squinted at him suspiciously. "What are you getting at?"

"We don't need a sheepdog. We need a sloth dog! And you're perfect for the job. You've only got to herd them down the hill."

"What? Have you seen the size of those things? One kick and I'm done for."

"No way. Their front claws are far more powerful than their back legs. You're more likely to be gouged to death."

"You're not helping," Ivy growled.

"No, what I meant is that you shouldn't come at them from the front. Run around behind them. The wind is blowing down the mountain. It will carry your scent to them. Once they smell you, they'll move farther down the hill. All you have to do is bark at them and continue moving down the hill and they'll run back to the village."

The dire wolf shook her body from her head all the way to her tail. Her tail curled upward and Ivy pranced forward. "Okay. Let's give it a try."

She picked her way through the underbrush and darted off. Angus lost sight of her within seconds. He was pleased with himself. Once again, he had been dropped into a foreign world and he was using his brain to figure it out. There was nothing he couldn't do! He flopped proudly in his snowshoes back down the trail.

The sound of distressed lowing and the vibration of the cedar trees alerted him that he hadn't exactly thought of absolutely everything.

And then the dire wolf began baying aggressively and pandemonium broke out. Angus looked down the narrow trail girded by trees on both sides.

He looked up the trail at the herd of ten to fifteen foot tall beasts frantically barreling their way down the tiny path. His eyes scanned the forest looking for an escape route. With a yell of shocking realization that he was about to be trampled to death by a bevy of overgrown possums, he lifted his knees to his chest and raced down the trail slapping the snow with his pine bough snowshoes.

The sloths' bellowing, Ivy's barking, and the deafening sound of blood beating in his frantic ears spurred Angus forward. His legs pounded the ground in a steady stride. His arms pumped with mechanical precision. He pulled the frosty air into his lungs and exhaled in an unbroken rhythm. The forest trail opened to the snow-covered grasslands outside of the village. Angus moved out of the way of the path and rested his hands on his knees. He bent over and gasped for breath.

After several minutes had passed, Angus looked to the trailhead. The sloths had not yet made their appearance. He had thought they were directly behind him. Where were they? He listened intently. Ivy's barks sounded far away now. Had the sloths evaded her?

He approached the trailhead and peered into the forest. Trees swayed about fifty feet up the trail. And then he saw the slow advance of the sloth column. They lumbered slowly forward, bellowing in fear. Each footstep was swallowed by heavy wet snow.

Unlike the dire wolf's paws, the sloths' claws did not spread over the snow. Every bit of their tonnage drove not only into the snow but squelched into the muddy earth beneath. In his panic to get away from the dumb brutes, Angus had neglected to observe their physical characteristics. He could have ambled slowly in front of them and been perfectly safe.

Angus jogged to the sloth corral and summoned several of the boys to help him. The boys spread out across the field and herded each of the giant animals into the pen as they appeared one-by-one at the bottom of the trail. Ivy brought up the rear and ran from one side of the field to the other, barking ferociously to move the few stragglers toward the boys. After the last sloth had been shut securely into the corral, Ivy trotted over to Angus.

"Great work!" Angus patted her head. She bared her teeth, raised her hackles, and nipped at him.

"Ouch!" He yanked his hand back. "Good thing I'm wearing a mitten. You could have hurt me!"

"Would have served you right! Do you always go around patting people on the head? It's insulting!"

"Sorry. It's just that you look so much like a dog."

Ivy snarled.

"Sorry," mumbled Angus right before lurching forward precariously.

"Gus! Brilliant idea having your pet herd the beasts into the corral." Billy thumped him soundly on the back. "Who knew you could train a wolf to work alongside humans?"

"Yeah, she's really smart," agreed Angus.

"Thanks," said Ivy out of the side of her mouth.

"The two of you are a good team," agreed Granny walking toward them. "Why don't you go home and get some lunch? Check back with me later. I may have another job for you."

She watched Mommy weave. Brown yarn in, treadle, squish. Brown yarn in, treadle, squish. All that brown yarn grows into brown fabric. Brown coats. Brown pants. Brown hats. Brown. Brown. Brown. Everything brown. She hated brown.

The stranger's sneakers weren't brown. They were bright, colorful, and sparkly. They were beautiful. She held one in her hand and reverently fingered the hard, glittering stones. She knew where to get these stones. She'd followed him in there. Lots and lots of pretty, colorful stones.

She would get her own and be sparkly and colorful too. She'd surprise Gussy when he got back. When the mean stranger was gone.

Angus hurried back to the hut. He removed his snowshoes and strode inside, Ivy close at his heels. Bonnie brushed past them on her way out. The direwolf sat down and scratched frantically, first behind one ear and then behind the other.

"What's that doing in here?" asked Mother from her seat at the loom. Angus glanced around, not sure what she was referring to.

"That animal," clarified Mother.

Ivy was inspecting her foot. She sniffed and licked at it, then collapsed in a groaning heap in front of the fire.

"We're going to have some lunch," explained Angus.

"What we're going to have are fleas. That animal is infested with them."

Ivy whimpered and began gnawing at her midsection.

"She worked hard this morning. We both did. I couldn't have rounded up all the sloths without her. Can she at least stay for lunch?"

Mother rose from the loom's bench. She regarded Ivy with undisguised distaste. "Feed it outside." She handed Angus two bowls of stew and held the drape while he and Ivy hustled out the door.

Angus brushed snow from a pile of logs beside the door and sat on the makeshift bench. Ivy settled beside him in the snow. She lapped at her bowl. He gulped his soup and placed his empty bowl on the ground beside hers. She licked both clean.

"Do you see my snowshoes?" asked Angus.

Ivy craned her neck. "Did you leave them here?"

"I think so." Angus wrinkled his forehead. "I took them off before we went in for lunch."

He stood up and searched around the yurt. Ivy reluctantly abandoned the bowls to help him. When after ten minutes they had not found the snowshoes, Angus said, "Somebody stole them."

"Who would do that? Nobody in the village even knows what they are."

Angus and Ivy stared at each other and chorused, "Except for Bonnie."

Angus was indignant. "That stupid kid! The snowshoes don't belong to her! Who does she think she is, stealing my snowshoes! What gives her the right?"

"She's your sister, I mean Gus's sister. I think sisters tend to do that, take things that belong to their brothers."

"It's not fair! Annoying, irritating little thief!"

"She'll bring them back."

"But I need them now! I wanted to go back up this afternoon, search for the World Jumper, and get out of this world!"

"You can build another pair."

"It will take me too long. It will be too dark to see anything by the time I'm done."

"Then it looks like we'll have to wait until tomorrow."

Angus had been hoping to get away before he had to clean up sloth dung again. "She'd better not break them," he muttered.

Mother came out of the house dressed in her coat and boots. "Gus, I'm off to the meat house to help preserve the beast that was killed this morning. Please keep an eye on Bonnie until I'm back." She hurried off.

Perhaps it was because he was still fuming about Bonnie's theft. Maybe he was trying to remember where he had lost the World Jumper. It might have been the unfamiliar reference to a sister he'd only had for twenty-four hours. Whatever the cause, he hadn't heard a word Gus's mother had said.

16

Bonnie's Pet

Bonnie had never gotten there so quickly. She knew all the secret animal trails through the forest. Not for her the large human path to the plateau. The animals knew how to get places quickly and quietly. Just like her. And the snowshoes the stranger who looked like Gus had made were magic. She stripped them off and shimmied up her lookout tree near the clearing.

She watched the monster leave the cave, stretch, yawn, and head north. The regular time. Countless afternoons she and Gus had watched the monster together. It always ventured outside in the early afternoon.

But she and Gus had never ventured into the cave. Until that first time when Granny had almost found out. But that hadn't been Gus, had it? That had been the stranger who looked like Gus.

The monster would be gone for only a short time, but long enough for her to get what she'd come for. She would race like the wolf over the snow in the stranger's snowshoes. She would cross the plateau, enter the monster's lair, and get some of those shiny rocks. Then she'd be sparkly.

She slid down the tree like a squirrel and reattached the magic snowshoes. Her arms and legs pumped her across the windy expanse. She removed the snowshoes, placed them within the cave's opening, and hurried to one of the dimly glittering walls. She hadn't been able to get one of the stranger's hard gray tools out of his special belt, but maybe one of the crystals would be loose enough to wiggle out with her fingers?

She was running her hands over the bumpy walls when she heard it. A tiny sound at first. If she'd been talking or tapping at the hard surface she would have missed it. It sounded like crying. Like scolding. Like a tiny baby complaining. She followed the mysterious noise to the rear of the cave. The light barely reached that far. The sound was louder. The baby was noisier now.

She bent down and vaguely glimpsed grass, leaves, animal fur. And something else. The something that was crying at her. Begging her to help it. She reached down and picked up the ball of light brown fluff. It regarded her solemnly with glowing yellow eyes. A pink mouth opened into a small O and said, "Mew."

The crystals forgotten, Bonnie refastened the snowshoes and raced away across the plateau, over the animal trails, and to the village, her new pet wrapped securely in her fur coat.

"Angus, you almost fell into the fire! Go take a nap!" The dire wolf nudged his leg with her muzzle.

They had just returned home after a grueling afternoon of hauling feed, cleaning the sloth corral—Billy had neglected to show up; big surprise there—and repairing the fence. Actually, to be precise, Angus had.

Ivy had spent the afternoon snoring in a pile of snow while he'd labored. His previous life of math problems, research reports, and science projects had not prepared him for the physical demands of this paleolithic existence. He longed for the comfort of his laboratory. He needed to find the World Jumper, but he was too exhausted even to contemplate the hike through the forest.

He grunted, "Maybe a short nap before dinner." He stumbled to the sleeping room and collapsed on his pallet. He curled into a ball and was asleep within seconds.

"Gus! Wake up! Where's your sister?" He was shaken awake by his mother.

He blinked sleepily at her. No, that wasn't his mother. That was Gus's mother. It took him a moment to remember that he wasn't home; he was in a yurt in a frozen world populated by megafauna.

"Where is Bonnie?" she demanded.

What was she asking? Oh yes, the annoying little girl who was always following him around and getting into his stuff.

"I don't know. I was sleeping."

"I gave you one job. Look after your sister while I'm working. That's all."

Angus considered that for a moment. "She wasn't here," he said sitting up.

"I know she's not here. I looked for her and all I found was you, fast asleep, not watching her."

"No. I mean she wasn't here when I got back from helping Granny. The house was empty. Actually, I haven't seen her since lunch."

"Why didn't you tell me? You should have come and gotten me! It's been hours. The sun is setting. She could be anywhere by now!" Mother's voice was high-pitched, quick, frantic.

Angus remembered last night's sentry duty, the blood on the snow, the lion. If that little kid was out there alone after dark, he didn't want to think what might happen.

He raced to the door and jammed his feet into his boots. "I'll go look for her," he said grabbing his coat. Ivy trotted to his side.

Mother pushed past him to the doorway. "We'll go to Granny and have her put a search party together."

The curtain flapped open in Mother's face. She backed away quickly and cried out, "Bonnie!" She grabbed the little girl in her arms, hugged her tightly, and twirled her around. She balanced her on a hip and then grew stern. "Where have you been, you naughty girl? I've been worried sick about you! You know you're not to wander off on your own!"

The little girl wrapped her arms around her mother's neck and cooed, "I'm sorry I worried you, Mommy. I was playing on the other side of the village." She stuck her tongue out at Angus over her mother's shoulder.

Angus peered outside into the gloom. His snowshoes were propped against the side of the hut, next to the doorway. At first glance, they appeared to be none the worse for wear. He pulled the drape closed against the cold and removed his boots and coat. Mother was bustling around the fire, preparing a fresh pot of stew for dinner. Bonnie had stripped off her outer garments and was warming herself by the fire.

The dire wolf was rifling through Bonnie's discarded clothes, sniffing as though she was trying to inhale them, and whining nervously.

She backed away from the little girl's coat, hackles raised and lips rolled back in a snarl.

"What is it?" whispered Angus.

Ivy turned, tail between her legs, and cocked her head at Angus. He followed her to the sleeping room and asked quietly, "What's wrong? What did you smell?"

She growled softly. "Lion."

Below the hut, out of earshot, the kitten was mewing.

Throughout dinner Angus watched Bonnie intently. Where had she been all afternoon in his snowshoes? Why did her clothing smell like lion? She spooned one mouthful of stew in after another, seemingly oblivious to his stare. Had she done something dangerous? Gone somewhere she shouldn't? She was a little kid. She could have been hurt.

He should have watched out for her better. Or at all. A sharp pang of remorse shot through him, an unfamiliar feeling. Guilt, fear, and an intense desire to protect the annoying little creep competed with the urge to yell at her for being so reckless and impulsive. Impulsive, like Angus himself. A family resemblance?

"Okay, you two. I want you to go right to sleep. We all had a very late, exciting night yesterday and we need our sleep," said Mother. "No arguments," she added needlessly as both the children retired to their pallets.

Ivy stood by the door whining. "And you can sleep outside," said Mother. "Probably have fleas all over my house as it is." She cleared away the bowls and pushed aside the drape for the dire wolf.

Ivy wandered a small distance from the hut and relieved herself. She lifted her nose to the air and breathed. A faint odor of enemy drifted on the air. She heard soft voices in the distance. The sentries were chatting at the gate. She didn't sense danger but where was the smell coming from?

She walked back toward the yurt. The cat smell grew stronger but it was sweeter than Ivy had remembered. The odor was confusingly non-threatening. No matter. It was a dark night and she was ready for a snack. She dug a tunnel under the fence and crawled through.

In the distance a distraught mother searched for her child. A deep, guttural wail echoed through the forest.

17

Cruising with Granny

Gus braced his legs against the dashboard and gripped his seat so tightly his knuckles ached. He was inside one of the strange, shiny animals. It was called a *car* and what they were doing was called *driving*. Trees, houses, and other cars swept past at a dizzying rate. He was definitely not enjoying this hallucination.

"I don't know what you got into this morning, young man. You had your parents in such a state. But you're with me now, so you'd better keep your behavior in check." Without warning Granny turned the steering wheel and the black car sped up a ramp. A horn blared behind them.

Gus had thought they were driving quickly before. His stomach lurched as they entered the wide road traveled only by other cars. No animals, no humans, nothing but shiny cars and trucks racing past each other. His hands grew wet and clammy as his mouth went dry. A close encounter with the monster might frighten him, but at least in such a case he'd be able to run or fight. His life would be under his own control. Of course, he reminded himself, he was only dreaming. The fever might kill him, but this dream wouldn't.

Granny swerved and crossed two lanes of traffic in less than one minute. Gus clamped his eyes shut and wished for another dream. Something relaxing, like being caught in the middle of a mammoth stampede. Anything but this horrifying *driving*.

"What do we need? Spinach, bacon, red onion, I think I have vinegar at home." The old woman recited a list of items while entering the highway. She let go of the steering wheel with one hand and fiddled with a knob. A loud voice boomed through the car.

Gus threw his hands over his ears and tried to turn to see who was talking. The seat belt dug into his shoulder. He was as motionless as that small monster he'd snared in his room last night.

He still didn't understand why Mother had been so angry with him. He had found the offspring of the monster that had been killing their sloths sleeping in his room. It had hissed and growled at him, spit in his face, and tried to scratch him. He had tied it up before heading off for sentry duty. He hadn't wanted the vicious creature to attack any member of the family while he was away so he had incapacitated it.

He could have understood if she'd been angry with him for keeping it alive. But she had insisted he "leave the cat alone." She'd even gone so far as to name the wretched thing. She called it Sir Schnortle.

Both Mother and Father were harboring it in the family home. Imagine! The monster finally slain and his parents fostering its young. What were they thinking? The animal needed to grow only a little larger and Bonnie would be in danger.

Gus missed his little sister. He missed her following him around, repeating everything he said, copying everything he did. Gus was her hero, even more than their father who was away on the hunt so often, and Gus knew it. She would do anything he asked, and consequently, he would do anything for her.

When Gus had finished his bath, and what a glorious bath it had been, water pouring hot from the *tap*, no need to melt snow or haul water from the well, what a wonderful dream, Granny had been waiting for him in the kitchen. No Bonnie.

Granny had given him a strange look when he'd asked about his sister. Mother had said that

Bonnie was safe with Granny. So where was she? He had seen the look pass between Mother and Father. They were keeping something from him, he knew. But when he'd pressed them, Mother insisted that Bonnie was fine and told him he shouldn't worry about it. She hustled him into Granny's car.

Drums beat in his ears: Strange and various sounds, animal voices perhaps, combined with a man's voice. The man was keening and wailing, complaining about a woman, a lost love.

"What is that?" asked Gus. He felt the drums thumping in his back, vibrating his feet on the floor.

"Oh, do I have the radio turned up too loud? Sorry, I like this song." Granny twisted a knob and the drums subsided but the wailing continued.

"What is that?" repeated Gus. "Who is it?"

"You don't like this song? Or don't you feel like country music today?" Granny glanced at him quickly before turning her eyes back to the road. "Change the station if you want. But no rap. My old ears can't take that."

Gus hesitated, unsure what she was telling him to do. "Go ahead. Second dial on the right."

Gus twisted the knob as he'd seen her do. The sounds grew louder. "That's the volume, Angus. Second dial."

He twisted the first dial back and touched the second dial. As he rotated the knob, symbols lit up on a display and the sounds changed. Sometimes he heard a nondescript buzzing, sometimes speaking voices, sometimes strange sounds combined with voices ... *music*.

When he had turned the knob all the way to the left, he heard it. Beautiful, mellifluous tones filled the car. He needed to hear more. He turned the left knob and the music got louder. He settled back into the seat and closed his eyes. The music crashed over him. For a few moments he forgot he was racing over a highway in a transparent animal and still unsure whether his little sister was dead or alive.

"Mozart? Now I've seen everything." Granny leaned on the horn and shouted out the window, "What are you thinking? Share the road! Maniac!"

18

Thievery

The dire wolf's ears pricked to attention as footsteps crunched in the snow. She winked open one eye and watched a furry Bonnie exit the hut in the early morning light. She was clutching a chunk of dried meat in one hand.

Ivy raised her head from her paws and asked, "Where are you going so early?"

Bonnie gasped. When she realized it was Ivy's voice that had startled her, concern replaced the fear in her eyes. "Oh, poor Pet. Did Mommy make you sleep out here all night?"

"It's okay. I have thick fur."

"But it's so cold. And your family is inside. You shouldn't sleep all by yourself out here. Come on, I'll let you in."

"Your mother is worried about the fleas."

"We get more fleas from these fur coats and the stinky beasts than from you. That's no reason," said Bonnie.

Ivy rose stiffly to her feet. "Really, it's okay."

"Mommy treats you so badly. You are such a help to us. And not just to our family. To all of us in the village. She shouldn't make you sleep outside."

Ivy growled deeply in her throat. The little girl was absolutely correct. There was no reason she shouldn't sleep indoors.

"Come on inside. You can curl up in front of the nice warm fire before Mommy wakes up." Bonnie held the curtain open. Ivy thought she wouldn't mind thawing her bones before breakfast. The dire wolf entered the hut quickly before the girl could change her mind.

"Shhh." Bonnie lay her index finger across her small, rosy lips. "Don't wake up Mother." She closed the door.

Ivy grunted and settled down in front of the smoldering coals. It occurred to her that Bonnie hadn't told her where she was going, but it was early so the sentries would still be on duty and the gates to the village would be closed. Ivy had been up all night tracking rodents and didn't want to wake up yet. She assured herself that Bonnie couldn't get into too much trouble. But as she lay there lazily dozing, she thought of the lion she'd smelled on Bonnie's clothes last night and later when she'd been outside. She groaned, reluctantly rose from the cozy fireside, and approached the pallet where Angus was sleeping.

"Pssst, Angus," she whispered, not wanting to wake Mother. He pulled the woven blanket over his head and let out a snort.

She nudged his body with her head. "Angus, wake up." He rolled to his side, faced away from her, and farted loudly. Ivy sneezed and pawed at her nose. "Yuck! Angus!"

She nipped at the blanket and pulled it from his body. He flailed out an arm and nearly struck her across the nose. He was still sound asleep.

"This calls for drastic action," sighed Ivy. She stepped on to the pallet and licked his face from top to bottom. Angus sat bolt upright and wiped frantically at his face. Ivy dragged her tongue across the blanket to get the taste out of her mouth. They looked at each other in disgust.

"What'd you do that for?" he asked accusingly.

"Shhh! Don't wake Gus's mom. Bonnie's outside. I don't know what she's doing. I think you should go check."

"What do I care what she's doing? I'm not responsible for her." Angus grabbed the blanket from Ivy, shook it out, and wrapped it around himself.

"Remember the lion smell? I smelled it again last night. Outside."

"What does that mean? The lion's in the village?"

"Can't be. The sentries would have sounded the alarm. It's not exactly the kind of thing they'd miss. I don't know what Bonnie's up to, but she is your sister, or your alter's sister anyway. She could get into all sorts of trouble."

"True." Angus stood and grabbed his blue jeans. Mother had folded them and placed them neatly beside his pallet after they had dried. The dire wolf left the room to give him privacy while he dressed.

He put his legs into the jeans and pulled. The denim had shrunk and wrinkled as it dried. Angus jumped and tugged at the waistband to pull the jeans on. He heard something hard jangling in his pockets. He buttoned and zipped the jeans and shoved his hands into the pockets. He'd forgotten all about the crystals he'd stuffed in there the first day he'd arrived.

Angus strode to the table in the main room and spread out the collection from his pocket on the table. He sorted them by color. There were several large, clear stones.

"Angus? Could you hurry up? Who knows where Bonnie's gone."

"Huh? Oh, I got distracted. Sorry." Angus left the crystals on the table and walked to the doorway. The curtain flapped open and Bonnie entered the hut. She ignored Angus, took off her coat and boots, and returned to bed. Ivy detected a sharp, sweet smell as she passed.

Breakfast was a stew of nettles and some grain that resembled barley. Angus had trouble getting it down and once it was, he had trouble keeping it there. Gus's mother had little sympathy for him.

"I had planned to make chipped meat and gravy, but your pet ate our last piece of dried meat. I don't know who let it in after I went to bed." Her accusing eyes bored into the dire wolf.

Even though Ivy knew she was innocent of the theft, she couldn't help but stare miserably at the ground. From time to time she peeked up at Bonnie who sat innocently slurping her breakfast.

A blast of cold air ruffled Ivy's fur as the door opened and Granny entered. "Good morning, all!" she called cheerfully.

"You're in a good mood this morning," said Mother, ladling a helping of stew into a bowl.

"Quiet night, deep sleep, great weather today. What's not to be happy about?" said Granny.

"No monster last night?"

"No. Strange though. We thought it would be back to finish the job it started. Because Gus's pet prevented it from making off with our beast, we figured it would be back to hunt again. The sentries heard it in the forest, but it never approached the village."

"Maybe it's afraid of Ivy," suggested Angus. He grinned at the dire wolf. She was still sulking about Mother's false accusation and ignored him.

Bonnie finished her meal before the others. She put her dirty bowl on the table for Mother to clean. Nobody saw her scoop Angus's carefully sorted crystals from the table into her pocket.

19

The Hunters

"So where are we really going, Angus?" Angus and Ivy were climbing the hill through the forest. After breakfast Angus had told Mother that he and Ivy were going to hunt squirrels, yet Angus had neglected to bring a weapon.

"To get the World Jumper."

"Do you remember where you lost it?"

"I need to retrace my steps. I came into this world on a plateau beyond the forest. I noticed it was missing when I was up there. It must still be up there."

"Sounds simple enough."

"One thing you should know. When Granny found me up there, she kept mentioning the so-called monster."

"Do you think the lion lives up there?"

"Or hunts up there. In any case, we need to be alert."

Angus and Ivy walked up the trail. Ivy trotted along nose to the ground, crisscrossing the trail like a nervous bloodhound.

"I'm sure I didn't drop it in the forest. You don't honestly think you can smell a barcode scanner all the way from here, do you?" Angus asked incredulously.

"Of course not. I'm hoping to find a squirrel for lunch."

The two reached the grove of trees at the top of the ridge. Ivy gazed forlornly at the expansive windswept plateau. The wind played with the snow, blowing it in whirling eddies, scraping it from the frozen ground in one place and piling it in great drifts in another place.

"That's a vast area. How are we ever going to find the World Jumper?" she whined.

"Let's check out the cave first," said Angus.

"Cave?" asked Ivy.

"I think I dropped it in there. When Bonnie knocked me down."

"Cave?" she repeated.

"If it's not in the cave we'll have no choice but to wander over the bluffs searching snow drifts."

"What cave?" yelled Ivy.

"Oh, I didn't tell you about the cave I found?"

Ivy lifted a lip in a silent snarl.

"So, I found a cave."

"Don't think I won't take a bite out of your leg."

"Come on, I'll show you."

They had reached the plateau. Angus lifted his knees high and jogged across the top of the snow. He barreled headlong into the rough wind and was glad for his snowshoes. He crossed the snow-covered expanse quickly, reached the outcropping, and walked northward searching for the gap in the rocks. Snow lay piled on top of the logs he had gathered two days ago.

"Right here, Ivy!" He waved his hand and she scrambled over the rocks and followed him through the opening.

Angus clicked on his penlight and shone it around the cave.

"Wow!" Ivy breathed as she took in the illuminated interior and sparkling, polychromatic walls.

"It's awesome, isn't it?" Angus spun around happily spreading his arms wide in a grand, proud gesture. "Do you like my cave?"

"Your cave?" Ivy lifted her nose into the air, took several small whiffs, and then inhaled once, deeply. "This is her cave!"

"Whose cave?" asked a perplexed Angus dropping his arms to his side.

"The lion's cave. This must be her lair. She was here recently. I don't know how long we've got until she returns."

"How do you know she's not here?"

"Easy. We're still alive."

Angus gulped. "We'd better search quickly."

"What are these?" asked Ivy, peering through a particularly large clear crystal jutting from the wall.

Angus giggled. "Your nose looks huge!"

Ivy growled. "All the better to smell you with, my dear."

"No, I mean it's bigger than usual. The crystal magnifies it. Look!" Angus pulled a small hammer from his toolbelt and tapped gently at the crystal until it broke free from the wall. He held it to his eye. The dire wolf snorted.

"It looks like you have one giant eye," she said. She sniffed the wall and touched a blue crystal with her tongue. "This one makes everything seem blue."

"It's fluorite," explained Angus chipping the blue crystal from the wall. "It's a colorful mineral often used for jewelry. It can be purple, blue, green, yellow, orange, pretty much any color of the spectrum." He trained his flashlight on a green, and then a purple, crystal before chiseling them from the wall and popping them into his coat.

"But that first one was clear."

"Yes. That's also a possibility. In my world, scientists have used transparent fluorite for microscope and telescope optics." He held the large, clear crystal to his eye and peered through it. "This one is special though. It has a tiny defect deep inside the crystal. It seems to be something metallic. That's very unusual."

"Explain," demanded the impatient dire wolf.

Angus wandered around the cave's perimeter while telling Ivy about the crystals. "Lenses made from fluorite tend to exhibit less chromatic aberration than those made from glass. Chromatic aberration is what you see when light passes through a glass prism and sheds a rainbow of colors. There are different wavelengths of light and when they shine through glass, you sometimes see weird colors at the edges. Fluorite is special because it doesn't break down the light as much as glass does."

He edged toward the rear of the cave. "There are two interesting things about this cave. First of all, in my world you don't typically find so many different colorations of fluorite in one place. Secondly, fluorite crystals without optical defects are not that big. That's why our scientists only use them for tiny optical elements like those in microscopes.

"This one is special." He rotated the large stone in his hand. "There's something about that piece of metal." He tucked the large piece of fluorite securely into his coat.

"This is all very interesting, but let's not forget what we came here for," urged Ivy.

"Oh, yeah. Distracted again. Sorry."

Angus thought about where he'd been when Bonnie had shoved him. He focused the penlight on the floor and moved it slowly from side to side until he reached the rear of the cave. He saw a dark mass not far from where he'd stumbled.

"There! There it is! Got it!" yelled Angus, stuffing the World Jumper into his fur coat beside the large piece of fluorite. "What's this?"

The dire wolf glanced up from the rose crystal she was regarding. She loped toward him. "What do you see?"

"It's hard to tell. It's shoved into a dark crevice. It almost looks like—a nest. Ivy, why would a lion have a nest?"

The penlight flickered and went out. Angus whacked it against the heel of his hand. "Great. Battery's dead." He shoved the flashlight back into his toolbelt. If not for the glimmer from the cave opening penetrating the gloom, Angus and Ivy would have been plunged into total darkness.

Ivy sniffed the air again. "Funny. That smells faintly of, hmmm."

Angus inhaled deeply but was thwarted by the gamey odor of his own sloth coat. "What do you smell?"

"Something was in here. There's a sweet smell." Ivy began to drool and licked her chops. "A yummy, young smell." In the gloom, her eyes glinted alarmingly.

Suddenly, the cavern went completely dark and a high-pitched, screeching yowl pierced the air. Angus and Ivy spun toward the cave entrance. The light sprang through as the lion cleared the aperture. The dire wolf's hackles raised, tail extended straight upward. Ivy snarled menacingly at the approaching lion.

"Run!" she barked at Angus. He scooped a handful of crystals and stones from the cave floor and raced toward the opening.

The sounds of a fierce battle reverberated off the hard, cold, crystal walls. Angus had one leg outside the cave when he heard a blood stopping yelp. He squeezed to the side to allow some light to enter and saw that the lion held the dire wolf by the throat.

A primal scream erupted from Angus's throat and he launched the stones as hard as he could at the lion's powerful head. They bounced ineffectually off the feline's right shoulder and scattered, but it was enough to get the animal's attention. No longer considering the dire wolf a threat, the lion released Ivy and sprinted at Angus.

Angus scrambled from the cave and fell over the rocks. He fled across the snow, thankful once again that he'd had the foresight to construct snowshoes. He looked over his shoulder and saw the lion emerging from the cave and searching for him. Adrenaline coursed through his veins as he realized the powerful animal was going to give chase. Snowshoes or not, there was no way he could possibly outrun the primeval beast.

He faced forward again in time to watch his snowshoe catch on a protruding rock. He screamed as his body was propelled forward. Instinctively he threw his arms out to cushion his fall and he slid down the rocky ravine, his body alternately rolling and bouncing down the slope, the sloth fur becoming encased in wet, heavy snow along the way. His head smacked against a rock and his body ground to a stop at the bottom of the ravine.

The dire wolf had dragged itself bleeding from the cave. The lion had let it live, but barely. It took every ounce of stubborn will Ivy had left to pull her injured body through the snow, inch by painful inch, into the shelter of the trees. She knew the blood trail was an invitation for the lion to come finish the job. But what difference did any of it make now? She had watched Angus fall off a cliff. Her low, plaintive howl sounded from the forest.

20

The Grocery Store

Gus had never seen so much meat in one place. Sure, after a successful mammoth hunt there was meat hanging everywhere, drying and curing. But this was fresh pink meat and a variety of animals. What was a *beef* anyway? For that matter, what was a *pork*? Can you drool in a hallucination? He wondered if his unconscious self would drown in his own saliva.

His grandmother reached out and grabbed a package of something that looked like mammoth jerky. "Bacon, for the salad," she explained.

"Come along, Angus. I need to buy some spinach."

Gus obediently turned and followed her. This food hut was huge. Everywhere he looked were boxes with strange symbols stacked on shelves, jugs of variously colored liquids, and open cases blowing wintery air and packed full of food-like items. The hut was so big that humans pushed large shiny wheelbarrows stuffed full of the foods.

Gus was confused. "When was this food hut built?"

"Oh, doesn't your mom shop here? It's nice, isn't it? I think they finished construction on it a year ago this spring. Still looks new."

Sometime in the middle of the night, shortly after he'd tied up the *cat* and grabbed his spear, Gus had realized this was the deepest dream he'd ever had. He was trapped in a disorienting fog from which there was no escape. And Bonnie was on his mind every second.

"I'll get the spinach," said Granny. "Would you please grab me a red onion? On second thought, make it two."

Gus looked at the bins full of colorful plant pieces. His grandmother was sorting through leaves. Perhaps she needed some fodder for the sloths, but with the monster gone, they should be able to let the animals graze again. He wasn't sure what a *red onion* was or why the sloths would need two of them. There were many red things in these bins. He looked for the reddest plants he could find, and grabbed the largest two. He placed them in the shiny wheelbarrow.

Granny glanced up. "Why did you put pomegranates in the shopping cart? I didn't know you liked those."

Gus reached in to the *shopping cart* to retrieve them, but Granny took them from him and put them back in the cart.

"That's okay. I'm happy to buy them for you. Don't forget my onions though. Red, remember? The yellow ones are too sweet."

Gus scanned the bins again. Here was a clue. *Onions* came in both red and yellow. Which of these plants had two colors? He saw them immediately. They looked nothing like the *pomegranates*. He picked up two red ones, avoided the yellow ones, and put them in the cart.

"Angus," said Granny. "Your mother needs to have more fruit in the house, I think. Why don't you put a few pounds of those apples in a bag? I'll buy them for you."

Gus stood stupidly blinking at his grandmother. "The bags, right here. These green plastic ones. Pull them like this, and then rip them apart." Granny showed him how it was done. "Don't you ever go shopping with your mother? Honestly, kids today are bilingual and play the piano before they can walk, but have no idea how to do something simple like bag a few apples."

Gus rolled his eyes. "I saw that!" said Granny. Gus filled a bag with apples and put it in the cart. "Did you weigh them?" she asked. "Give them to me."

She snatched the bag out of the cart and plunked it on a large shiny device. Gus watched as the device sank under the weight of the apples and a black arm moved around a circular face with more strange symbols.

"See?" she said. "Four, and almost a half, pounds. Now I'll have an idea how much they're going to cost me." She removed the bag and the device popped up while the black arm dropped to the left.

Curious, Gus pushed the device down and watched the arm move slowly up and to the right. He let go and the arm winged back to the left with a loud *pong*.

"Angus! Quit playing with the scale! Honestly, anyone would think you're five!" Granny pushed the cart. "Come along! Oh drat, we forgot the onions." She scurried back and grabbed two round balls with peeling skin. Their evil acidic odor assaulted Gus's nose when she dropped them into the cart. In his opinion, they were most certainly not red.

Gus's first excursion into a grocery store continued like this. Granny asked him to retrieve something, he brought back something entirely different, and the shopping cart's contents grew.

And then in the frozen food section somewhere between ice cream and shelled peas, it happened. The prim old stranger wasn't dressed for a day of grocery shopping. Her pearl necklace, floral dress, and polished and pointy shoes indicated she had stopped briefly on her way to or from a more fashionable engagement.

She adjusted the straw hat on her head. She was an avid crafter and an amateur fashion designer, and her creativity had exploded all over this hat. She had attached the leaves, berries, and plastic flowers herself with her hot glue gun. The addition of the bird had been sheer inspiration but did make the hat a trifle unbalanced.

She pushed her shopping cart slowly along, peering through the closed glass doors until she found the diet dinners. She stopped to compare prices and calorie counts when a war whoop shouted into her right ear caused her to clutch her chest and sink to the floor.

Standing in line at the checkout with his grandmother, Gus had seen the fashionable older woman enter the store. He watched her stride purposefully toward the frozen food section. He had seen her stand indecisively in front of the closed freezer doors. He had known that every moment counted.

He raced to her side, roared his most ferocious roar, and grabbed the hat from the gasping woman's head. He whacked it into the freezer doors, once, twice, three times. The glue held tightly to the leaves and berries. He tossed it to the floor and began stomping and jumping on it.

"Die! Die!" he yelled.

Still, the plastic flowers clung to the hat. He reached down, grabbed the bird, tore it from the hat, and ran with it to the front of the store. The automatic doors sensed him and opened to the outdoors. With all his might, Gus threw the bird into the parking lot and raced back to the speechless and gasping woman cowering in the frozen food aisle.

He reached down and respectfully helped her to her shaking feet. "Are you okay, ma'am? That vulture almost ate your brain."

The cashier paused a moment from scanning a box of cereal and smiled at Angus's mortified grandmother. "Well, in his defense, it was a hideous hat."

21

Angus Mounts Up

Hot air puffed at Angus's closed eyelids. The not entirely unpleasant stink of rotted leaves drifted up his nostrils. A gentle poking at his cheeks and forehead grew more insistent. One of his eyelids was pulled rudely open and he woke grumbling.

He realized he had the worst headache of his life. He grabbed his head and moaned. He squinted his eyes gingerly open and saw a thick black hose dangling above his forehead. He attempted to focus his blurry vision and succeeded only in crossing his eyes.

The hose waggled to and fro and then curled upon itself in an alarming manner. Angus gasped and tried to raise his head to get away from what must be some weird black snake. Pain sliced through his head cutting from ear to ear, and he squeezed his eyes shut again.

His head hurt so badly he didn't much care if the bizarre snake bit him with venomous fangs or squeezed all the breath from him before devouring him whole. Just make the throbbing stop! When instead of the expected strangulation or poisoning he felt a soft brushing against his cheek, he dared to open his eyes again. This time they were better able to focus on the snake-hose-thing. It wiggled around to the top of his head and removed his safety goggles.

"Hey!" he complained and grabbed at it. It dropped the safety goggles on to his chest and squeezed his hand. He yanked his hand back sharply.

Gritting his teeth through the pain, Angus rolled to his stomach and raised himself to his knees. He took a deep breath and vomited. It felt like his brain was exploding inside his skull. Something pulled the fur hood from his head and stroked him through his hair. And then Angus noticed the enormous hairy foot standing directly beside him.

"Aaaah!" yelled Angus. He rolled away from the monstrous foot and bumped into its twin. He turned his head painfully toward the sky and stared up at a twitching proboscis.

"A mammoth!" gasped Angus.

"No, actually a mastodon," said the mastodon. "I do look similar to a mammoth, but I'm not closely related. I have shorter legs, a longer body, and more muscles than a mammoth. My teeth are different from a mammoth's also. More suited to chewing leaves and branches of trees and shrubs. My kind lives in forests and woodlands. I believe mammoths prefer grasslands."

"Enough with the natural history lesson! Where's the lion?" Angus grabbed his fallen goggles, checked to be sure his toolbelt and the World Jumper were intact, and tried to scramble to his feet. He collapsed again, heaving on the snow.

"Careful, careful," soothed Ivy. "You had a very nasty fall off the cliff up there and, from the knot at the back of your head, I can tell you whacked yourself pretty good, too."

"We need to get out of here! What if the lion finds us?"

"Easy there. I don't think we've got to worry about her while I'm in this body. She's not going to attack a huge, healthy mastodon. Too dangerous. I could cause her some serious bodily damage. You're safe with me."

Angus rested his head in the cold, numbing snow and closed his eyes.

"And the dire wolf?"

"Bleeding a short ways from here. I went as far as I could in its body but jumped as soon as I saw the mastodon herd. I had to get to you."

"Is it dying?"

"I don't think so."

"Then we have to help it."

"After we help you. Do you think you can climb onto my back?"

Angus sat up slowly. The mastodon looked anxiously down at him. "How? I've ridden a horse once or twice, but they've all had stirrups and saddles. I've never ridden bareback. How will I get up there anyhow?"

"Can you stand?"

Angus rose shakily. He wobbled and Ivy grabbed his elbow with her proboscis, steadying him. "Okay?"

Angus began to nod in the affirmative and instantly regretted the head movement. He grimaced and muttered, "Yeah."

"Here's something you don't hear every day," began Ivy. "Step on my nose." She extended her proboscis, bending the end of it like a tiny step.

Angus grabbed it and pulled his body up to rest on it.

"Ow! Ow! Ow! Get off! GET OFF!" hollered Ivy. Angus thudded to the ground. He landed heavily on his bottom. Now both ends of him throbbed.

"What did you do that for!" he demanded angrily.

"I didn't realize that would hurt so much. It felt like you were pulling my nose clear off the front of my face. How much do you weigh?"

Angus ignored the question. "So how do you suggest I get on?"

The mastodon swung her proboscis back and forth. "I'll have to bend down and we'll have to find you something to climb up on." She looked around. "Plenty of boulders here. How about that one?"

Angus got to his feet and limped to the huge rock she had indicated with her proboscis. Maybe it was the same one that had knocked him unconscious. He stood on top of it. Ivy settled herself gingerly on the ground. First, she bent her front right and front left legs and knelt on them. Next, she bent her back left leg and finally her back right leg. Angus lay across her huge back and tried to straddle his legs across it.

"Ow! Your back is too wide. I can't ride you."

"Try to ride sideways."

"I'll fall off!"

"You can hold on to my ear."

"That will make me fall off more slowly. It won't keep me on."

"Are you suggesting we build a saddle? Out here in the middle of nowhere? With an angry, hungry lion on the prowl?"

"No. I'm just wondering if it would hurt you too much for me to sit on your neck."

"My neck!"

"It's a lot narrower. I could scoot myself up there. But what if I'm too heavy?"

"Okay. It would be easier than making a saddle. If it works. Be ready to get right off if you're too heavy!"

"Agreed." Angus shimmied forward and gently straddled the mastodon's neck. "Is that okay?"

"Not too bad. Don't squeeze with your legs though. Balance yourself with my ears. I'm getting up now. Hold on." Angus rocked forward as Ivy straightened her legs in the opposite order she had first folded them: back right leg, back left leg, then the front left leg and the front right leg.

"Still on?" she asked.

Angus wiggled his bottom until he was perfectly centered and answered, "Yes. Let's go."

The mastodon lumbered through the valley, and Angus swayed gently side to side on her neck.

"How are we going to climb back up to the top?"

"We aren't. We'll follow the valley around and come out on the other side of the village."

"How do you know that?"

"This body is telling me. It must be some route this mastodon travels with her herd. It's like I'm seeing a map in my head, and all I need to do is follow it."

"A paleolithic GPS!" Angus laughed and regretted it instantly as his head hammered.

"I left the dire wolf body somewhere around here. There she is!"

The injured animal lay in a heap. When they approached, it growled and raised its hackles.

"Do you think it will attack?" asked Angus. And then a miraculous thing happened. At the sound of his voice, the dire wolf whined, wagged its tail, and tried to stand.

"She recognizes you!" said Ivy. "And even more surprising, she seems to like you!"

"Hey, what's not to like," demanded Angus.

"She's a wild animal. She should either want to fight you or flee from you. For some reason, she trusts you."

"You trust me," said Angus. "Maybe she does because you did while you were in her body."

The mastodon considered this for a moment. "Do you think the animal minds stay in the bodies when I body jump? That they share the body with me, like roommates?"

"That might explain why you have a map in your head right now. How about you let me off so I can check her out?"

Ivy lowered herself slowly and Angus rolled off. He hurried to the dire wolf's side and quickly examined the hurt animal. She yelped and growled as he probed her back leg, but she didn't bite him.

"I don't think anything's broken. Lots of flesh wounds. Maybe a pulled muscle. Some rest and she should heal up nicely."

"Great, Dr. Doolittle. Any idea how to get her back to the village?"

Angus pulled off his snowshoes and tethered them together. He prodded the wolf until she moved uneasily to the conveyance. After a bit of coaxing, she settled down upon it.

"Think you can pull her?" he asked Ivy.

The mastodon bent her head and reached for the sled. "I can reach it if I bend my head, but I can't walk all the way to the village like this."

Angus pulled the safety goggles from his head and untied the leather laces of his boots. He braided the laces and the elastic band of the goggles into a makeshift rope. He lashed the rope to the front of the sled. Next, he gripped the goggles and pulled, stretching the rope as far as it would extend, and then gave it to Ivy.

The mastodon gripped the plastic goggles and asked, "What if they break?"

"Then I fix them." He climbed back on to her neck and the three of them set off for the village.

22

Aches and Pains

On the trek back to the village, the shooting pain in Angus's skull subsided to a dull throbbing. Despite the nagging drumbeat between his ears, he couldn't keep himself from wondering why the lion hadn't attacked him as he lay defenseless at the bottom of the cliff.

Perhaps he'd been thinking out loud because Ivy suddenly said, "It's odd that the lion didn't chase you down the ravine."

"I was completely unconscious. She could have taken her time."

"And I wasn't there to help you," added the mastodon.

"So why didn't she kill me?"

"You know," began Ivy. She stopped midsentence and scratched her head thoughtfully with her proboscis. She picked up the cord and began dragging the wolf on the sled again before she continued her thought. "I saw you roll off that cliff. She was almost on you. When you went over, she stopped in her tracks. She looked a bit confused and wandered back and forth for a while. She was doing strange things, like pawing at her eyes and sniffing the air."

"You mean she was searching for me."

"Yes, it seemed so. But she had been chasing you. Surely she must have watched you go over the side."

"Then why didn't she follow me?"

Ivy thought about this. "It looked like she had lost you. She was sniffing for you, and maybe the snow you rolled in dulled your scent."

"She could have seen me if she'd looked. Even if I was covered in snow."

"But she didn't see you."

Angus chewed his lip as he realized how lucky he'd been to escape the lion. Now he understood why Granny didn't want him or Bonnie on the plateau. He heard the dire wolf growl from the sled. "Don't look now, but we've got company," said Ivy.

Angus looked over the mastodon's bulky head and saw the village in the near distance. The tiny figure of Bonnie was springing through the snow like an alpine rabbit. He groaned. "My headache just came back."

"Be nice," warned the mastodon.

"How did you get up there?" yelled the little girl as she approached. "Can I have a ride, too?"

"No!" said Angus.

"Angus!" hissed Ivy.

"Maybe later," he called down.

Bonnie ran to the sled. "Pet! What happened to Pet?"

"No! Watch out!" shouted Angus as Bonnie bent down to stroke the dire wolf. "That's not Ivy, not a pet!"

"Calm down, Angus. Look," soothed Ivy. The dire wolf was thumping its tail and whining happily. It appeared to recognize Bonnie. She stroked its head, singing softly to herself and cooing, "Poor Pet. You hurt yourself again. Don't worry, I'll take care of you." The dire wolf licked her chin.

"Amazing. She remembers you!" said Angus.

"Why wouldn't she? We're friends. Right Pet?" Bonnie waited for a response but the wolf merely gazed at her with adoring eyes. "Why doesn't she answer me?"

"Maybe she doesn't feel like talking right now," said Angus. He glanced up from Bonnie and the wolf and noticed villagers massing together outside the walls of the encampment.

"Ummm, Ivy, do you see what I see?" He spoke gently into the mastodon's ear. She had been watching Bonnie and the wolf also. She blew air loudly out her nose and stepped anxiously from hoof to hoof.

"You'd better get off quickly if you want to return to the village. I think it's in my best interest to leave you now. I have no desire to be tonight's dinner."

"They eat mammoth and sloth. Do you think mastodon is on the menu, too?"

"I think they aren't too choosy about where the meat comes from. Now, are you getting off?"

"Waiting for you to kneel down."

"No time. Slide around off the side."

Angus grabbed Ivy's neck and slid his left leg off the right side of her body. He dropped heavily to the ground. When she saw he had safely dismounted, the mastodon turned and stampeded back the way they had come.

The dire wolf shook its head. Angus looked quickly at the animal and noticed a spark come into its eyes.

"How does your head feel?" asked Ivy, safely inside the dire wolf's body once more.

"Like a woodpecker has mistaken it for a snag."

"Pet is talking again!" announced Bonnie.

"Think you can drag me the rest of the way to the village? I don't want to walk on this leg if I don't have to."

Angus grasped the makeshift sled handle and began to pull.

"Me, too!" demanded Bonnie.

For once, Angus didn't tell her she was too little.

23

A Light in the Crystal

The entire village had witnessed Angus riding on a mastodon. There was no denying it had happened. Granny and Mother were demanding an explanation.

"You could have been killed! You could have fallen off and been trampled to death!" scolded Mother.

Granny added, "It could have strangled you with its nose!"

Angus conceded that Mother's worries might have occurred, but rather significantly, didn't. However, the image of Ivy's proboscis wrapped around him like a boa constrictor crushing a jungle animal was too hilarious. Granny had not appreciated his outburst of laughter so now he found himself cleaning up sloth dung yet again, even though it was Billy Robert's turn. It seemed Angus was always scooping poop when it was Billy's turn.

He scooped the last stinking shovelful into the overloaded wheelbarrow and pushed it to the steaming compost heap. He stomped back to the hut, burst through the heavy drape, and glowered at the dire wolf snoring peacefully by the peat fire. A quick scan of the small abode revealed no one else at home. There was no door to slam spitefully so he threw his boot at the slumbering animal. Ivy jerked awake with a bark.

"Oh, it's you," she yawned. "Finished the job?"

"Next world, you get to be the human and I'll be the pampered pet."

Ivy grimaced as she stretched her injured back leg. "You don't know how much I'd like that. Does this mean we're moving on?"

Angus sniffed at the pot heating over the smoldering peat. He inhaled the heavy aroma of meat stew and his cheeks pricked as saliva started to flow. He was hungry! He dipped the bone ladle into the pot and served himself a bowl of the hearty meal. He quirked his eyebrow at the dire wolf.

"No, thanks. Bonnie gave me some earlier. So, what's the plan?"

Angus swallowed a gulp of the rich brown broth and munched a meat chunk before answering. "I've got to check the World Jumper to be sure there's no damage. I wish there was some way to know where we were headed so I could prepare myself. Arrive with the proper clothing at least."

Angus slurped more of the delicious salty liquid. It warmed him straight through. When he'd consumed all the broth, he broke apart the tender chunks of meat and popped them into his mouth one after another. He tossed one to Ivy who caught it before it touched the ground.

"Let's hope the next world is populated with animal lovers. That would be a refreshing change," she said, licking her chops.

Angus placed his empty bowl on the table. He removed his coat and searched its inner folds for the World Jumper. His fingers grazed loose pebbles. He'd almost forgotten the crystals he'd gathered. He extracted several beautiful, small bits of fluorite in a rainbow of shades. He shoved his hand deeper down in the pocket and pulled out the large, clear rock with the interesting metallic aberration. He plunked it beside the colored stones on the table. The World Jumper was the last thing he took from the coat. He placed it gently on the table among the rocks before hanging his coat on the hook by the door.

"Angus! Quick! It's glowing!" gasped Ivy. The dire wolf's ears were pressed flat against her head. She growled fearfully. Angus looked at the table. The clear crystal radiated a warm violet light from deep within its core. Angus was drawn to the table.

He touched the crystal tentatively. It felt cool. He picked up the crystal and regarded it. The light was immediately extinguished. He placed it beside the World Jumper. It lit up again immediately. He moved it away, and it went dark. The aberration in the rock was reacting with his invention.

He held the rock in his hand and turned it to catch the flickering light of the wall lanterns. His mind was reeling, trying to figure out what this discovery might mean. The door to the hut slammed, and he looked up.

"What's that there?" asked Granny as she strode across the room.

"Ummm, just a crystal," he stuttered and blocked the table with his body.

"Let me see," she demanded. He wordlessly handed her the large stone. While she examined it, he reached a hand behind his back and hid the World Jumper under his shirt. "Interesting," she said. "What are you hiding back there?"

"Nothing," he said and stepped from the table. While Granny looked at the pile of variously colored stones, Angus quickly handed the World Jumper to the dire wolf. Ivy hid the invention beneath her large paws.

"These are beautiful," said Granny picking up each stone in turn. "Where did you get them?"

"Lemme see!" demanded Bonnie, who had just entered the hut with Mother. "I know what those are! They're from ... ." She stopped abruptly.

Granny looked at her expectantly. "Well, child? Where did they come from?"

Bonnie and Angus stared at each other. Angus suddenly realized the adults didn't know about the cave. And Bonnie clearly didn't want them to know. This required further investigation. Angus invented quickly. "Billy traded them to me for taking his sentry shift. I don't know where he got them. Maybe his dad brought them back from a hunt?"

The explanation was accepted without question. Granny grunted. "That boy can find more ways to get out of an honest day's work." She returned the large rock to him and peered at the colorful crystals on the table. Mother joined her.

"May I look at one?" Mother asked. He nodded. She picked up a small, clear crystal and peered through it.

"Your face looks huge," observed Granny. She took the stone from Mother and held it to her eye. She inhaled sharply and scurried around the small room looking intently at everything through the crystal.

Angus watched Gus's grandmother spring around the room. Put her in a purple velour tracksuit, some running sneakers, and a pair of thick bottle glasses, and she would be a ringer for his own grandmother back home. She blinked a gigantic eyeball at him through the clear rock and it suddenly dawned on him. Granny needed glasses, and he would make them for her from fluorite!

24

Child Psychology

Sir Schnortle adored lazy afternoons. He sprawled on his back, his front leg stretched in the air. He bathed the paw until it was sufficiently moist and then wiped his face with it. When he was satisfied that the left side of his head was adequately clean, he stretched out his other front leg and licked it wet before bathing the other side. He collapsed, closed his eyes, and purred happily.

The screeching car tires on the driveway outside disturbed his content mid-purr. He lifted his head slightly and cocked an ear. Running sneakers stomped across the porch, the front door was thrown open so hard it banged into the wall, and a fuming gray-haired lady announced to no one in particular, "Never again!"

Sir Schnortle scrambled to his feet and scooted up the stairs and under the first bed he could find.

"What happened, Mom?" Mrs. Clark dried her hands on a kitchen towel as she approached the front hallway. Mr. Clark glanced up from his laptop.

Angus's grandmother glared with magnified eyes through her glasses. She opened her red-painted lips to say something, thought better of it, and clamped them together again. She pursed them tightly, and then threw her hands in the air.

"I've had enough for one day. You're on your own."

She stomped out of the house, passed a puzzled Gus on the porch, grunted at him, and climbed back into her shiny black convertible. Gus silently watched her sports car scream backwards down the driveway. It braked suddenly and raced up the driveway. The passenger door flew open, two paper bags were ejected, and the car rolled down the driveway again. It peeled out on to the quiet, residential street and squealed away.

Gus carried the bags into the kitchen. Mr. and Mrs. Clark silently watched the disappearing car, and then followed Gus into the house.

"Angus, we're waiting for an explanation," said Mr. Clark.

"This is an apple and this is a pomegranate," answered Gus, holding up one of each. "Don't confuse them with onions."

"Yes, Mom. Okay, Mom. Sorry, Mom." Mrs. Clark hung up the phone. She sighed and accepted a cup of tea from Mr. Clark.

"Is he asleep?" she asked.

"Yes. Door closed. Cat safely shut out."

"You know, I expected these in-between years to be a challenge. Trying to grow up can be difficult. They change so much on the way from little children to young adults. I've read all the books about that. But none of them tells you what to do when your mild-mannered son kidnaps your family pet," said Mrs. Clark.

"Or opens a butcher shop in your kitchen," added Mr. Clark.

"Or attacks an old woman in the grocery store." Mrs. Clark slumped into a chair.

"He was asking about Bonnie again. Wanted to know if she was dead."

Mrs. Clark shook her head. "What did you say?"

"I acted shocked. Said absolutely not. Said she was visiting family for a few days."

"Do you think she's a real person we've never heard of?"

"I don't know. She could be a figment of his imagination," suggested Mr. Clark.

"He didn't have an imaginary friend when he was four. I doubt he's invented one now," said Mrs. Clark.

"Maybe that's exactly what he's done. Invented one. Really, think about it. He's been beyond his years ever since before he could speak. Is he making up for lost time? Never got around to having an imaginary friend before, so he's decided to have one now?" asked Mr. Clark.

"Most ridiculous thing I've ever heard."

"Well, think about it. First he pretends he's a pirate. Insists we call him by another name."

"And gets himself suspended from school." Mrs. Clark bit her lip. "Now we're supposed to call him 'Gus'. I hate to admit it, but you may be on to something. The other kindergarteners played dress up. Angus refused to play along. He said the costumes were historically inaccurate."

Mr. Clark nodded. "Exactly. He completely skipped that pretending stage. It's supposedly so important for a child's development. Do you think he's regressing?"

"So what is he pretending to be now? A big game hunter?"

"Could be. I don't know. What do we do about it?"

Mrs. Clark drummed her fingers on the kitchen counter. "If it really is an essential part of his development and he missed it, I don't think we have a choice."

"You mean?"

"I think we have to play along."

25

Angus Makes Eyeglasses

"Angus! Pssst! Angus!" He pulled the covers over his head and ignored the voice. It couldn't be time to get up for school. He was too sleepy.

"Angus! Wake up!"

The covers were pulled rudely from his body, exposing his naked legs to the cold air. "Five more minutes, Mom," he whined, reaching blindly for the bedsheets. His hand touched something cold and wet and he opened his eyes. The dire wolf was nudging him awake with her nose. It didn't matter how long he'd been away from home, he still couldn't get used to waking in a strange place.

"What is it?" he asked Ivy.

"Shhh. Keep your voice down. Mother is still asleep. Bonnie snuck out again. She didn't know I was awake. I saw her steal food. I'm going to be blamed for it again. Where do you think she goes in the early morning?"

"You woke me up to tell me that? I was having the best dream. I mean, I wasn't having any dream. I was sleeping. I forgot I was stuck here. It was wonderful."

"Sorry, but I don't feel like being accused of thievery again! Not when I didn't do it!"

"Little Miss Perfect doesn't like getting in trouble. Poor wolfie."

Ivy growled. "I didn't say I was perfect. Just innocent. And don't you want to know what Bonnie's up to? She always comes back smelling like cat. Don't you find that even a little bit suspicious?"

Angus pulled on his blue jeans. They weren't as warm as the long underwear and leather pants, but they were more comfortable and felt like home. "I want to go home. She's not our concern. We have the World Jumper back. Once I test it, we can get out of here."

"I heard it again last night. It's coming closer to the village."

"What's that?"

"The crying. I heard it two nights ago when I was hunting. It was in the forest. It sounded like an animal grieving. Like it had lost a member of its pack. It sounded heartbroken. Last night I heard again, but I was in the hut sleeping by the fire. It must be closer. How else would I be able to hear it?"

"Ivy, I'm sorry if this sounds callous, but I don't see what difference it makes." Angus pulled the cabled sweater over his head, buckled on his toolbelt, and strapped his goggles to the top of his head. "Let's test the World Jumper and get out of here."

Angus rolled the furs into a ball and shoved them into a corner of the bedroom. "Where is it?" he asked.

"By the fire. I slept on top of it last night."

Angus tiptoed into the central room, picked the barcode scanner up off the floor, and stuck it into the waistband of his jeans. He picked up the large piece of fluorite and stuck it in a pocket. A faint light glowed through the denim.

"You've got it too close to the World Jumper. Someone will see," advised Ivy.

Angus tugged on the hem of the sweater and stretched it to cover his pockets. "Better?"

"Invisible."

The curtain fluttered open and Bonnie walked into the hut. She jumped when she saw Angus already awake. "Good morning, Bonnie," he said casually.

"Uh, good morning," she stammered.

Angus noticed a guilty look pass over her face. She covered it quickly with an artless smile. Ivy was right, he thought. Bonnie was up to something. But he told himself that he didn't care. If she left him alone, he would leave her alone. Bonnie hurried to the bedroom and crawled back under her furs.

"Do you see what I mean?" hissed Ivy.

Angus heard Mother begin to stir in her room. He stoked the fire for breakfast. "Yeah. But let's eat something and go test the World Jumper."

"I don't understand why you brought those silly sneakers along."

Angus and Ivy were hiding out in Billy's yurt. Billy's mother would be preserving meat all day, and Billy had been thrilled to trade his evening sentry shift for the use of his family's house. Angus figured if he got the World Jumper working, he'd be long gone before he'd have to fulfill his side of the bargain. He'd give Billy a taste of his own medicine. Angus smiled to himself.

"We don't want the adults to find out about the World Jumper. They won't understand. They're going to wonder what I've been up to all day. I thought while I'm testing the World Jumper, why not make Granny some eyeglasses?

It will be a good explanation for what I've been doing all day and help Granny see better."

"Why does she need to see? She'll just use that eyesight to kill more innocent animals."

"They're not all innocent, Ivy. She needs to be able to protect the village from predators."

"One person's predator is another person's family member," growled Ivy. "But why do you need the sneakers?"

"I'm going to use the rubber to craft eyeglass frames. I'll attach the pieces of fluorite to it."

"I don't understand what the fluorite is going to do."

"Remember how I told you that scientists in my world use fluorite for microscope optics? They don't use it for anything larger because the clear, unflawed pieces in my world are very small. The pieces I found are big and clear. Granny's eyes were magnified when she looked through them. I'll use the stones for lenses."

Angus sorted through the clear crystals and selected several that were of relatively equal size. He held up each to the small torches lighting the hut to check for optical defects within the stone. The first crystal he looked through split the light into a prism of color. He rejected it and selected another. The second one allowed the light to pass straight through.

He explained to Ivy, "I need to start with the best pieces of fluorite. Color distortion within the stone indicates flaws. Light changes speed as it moves from the air into the stone. The speed change bends the light. If I see many colors within the stone it shows me that there are different angles within the stone. Those will interfere with clear, undistorted vision."

He searched through the stones until he found another equally pristine specimen. When he found two of similar size and quality, he checked them outside in the daylight. Finally satisfied that these pieces of crystal were appropriate for Granny's eyeglasses, he placed them carefully on Billy's kitchen table and pulled his safety goggles over his eyes.

He reached into his toolbelt and pulled out a sharp knife he had purloined from the butcher hut.

Ivy opened her eyes wide when she saw the blade. "What will you do with that?"

"I'll cut the rubber soles off the sneakers."

Angus rubbed his hands together to warm them. The hut was chilly. The peat fire at Billy's house was covered and smoldering. Of course, Billy's mother had expected no one to be at home that day. Angus stoked the fire and replenished the fresh peat. It smoked briefly and then caught fire. The peat burned slowly and steadily.

Ivy grunted and collapsed by the fireside. She rested her head on her paws and allowed her eyes to fall shut. Soon, the gentle sound of snoring filled the hut.

Angus poked at the canvas with the knife tip. He had used steak knives and bread knives before but never a knife as sharp and unforgiving as this one. He wasn't allowed to touch any of the knives in the butcher block at home. On his last birthday, his dad had given him a multi-tool with a small whittling knife, but he'd forgotten it in the pocket of a pair of pants his mother had laundered, and the tiny nuts and bolts had been washed away rendering the tool useless within a week.

He remembered his dad telling him to cut toward his buddy, not his body. He took a deep breath, and pushed the blade into the canvas. He rocked the knife and pushed it away from him gently. The blade stuck in the tough fabric. He needed to apply more force. He pressed harder until he heard a dull tearing noise. He wiggled the blade again and pushed it forward. A hole was appearing along the rubber rim of the shoe.

He continued pushing, wiggling, and ripping. He felt a burning sensation on the heel of his hand and knew that a blister was beginning to form. When he was three quarters of the way around the sneaker, he put down the knife and used brute force to rip the rubber off the canvas.

He held a rubber sole in one hand and the purple rhinestone canvas hi-top in the other. Now what? How was he going to make eyeglasses out of this?

He placed the stones on top of the rubber sole and looked at them for a moment. He needed to fit the stones into the rubber. He placed the blade tip on the rubber and slowly sliced a straight line about two inches from the sole's edge. The knife, sharp as it was, only penetrated a few millimeters. Angus traced the small slice in the rubber with the blade a second time making a deeper cut. Again and again he traced the line.

After twelve cuts, the blade touched the table. Angus pushed his goggles to the top of his head, held up the strip of rubber, wrapped it around his face, and marked the location of each eye with a carpenter pencil from his toolbelt.

He placed the rubber strip on the table and sliced an X over each pencil mark, tracing and retracing until the knife had cut completely through the rubber. He poked the rocks through each X and held the strip up to his head again. He looked through the crystals and saw an enlarged room. The slumbering dire wolf was even bigger. The bowls on Billy's table were huge. Angus could even see clods of dirt by the doorway. The glasses were so powerful they were beginning to give him a headache.

As he removed them from his head, one of the crystals dropped to the floor. That wasn't going to work. He couldn't have Granny's lenses popping out of her glasses all the time.

Angus picked up the crystal and shoved it back into the rubber frame. He needed to glue the crystals to the rubber somehow. "Ivy!" he called.

The dire wolf jerked her head up and blinked. "Have you finished?"

"Almost." He held up the eyeglasses for her to see.

"Primitive. Do they work?"

"They magnify everything. But the lenses keep falling out. I'm thinking we need to make some glue like we did last time."

"That took hours! We don't have that kind of time. You're supposed to test the World Jumper today, and Billy's mother will be back by dinnertime."

"Do you have another idea? I have to keep the rocks from falling out."

Ivy cocked her head to one side and squinted her eyes in thought. The harder she tried to figure out a solution, the more she realized she didn't have an answer. The greater her realization of her complete inability to help Angus, the more agitated she became. The more agitated she became, the more she twitched her tail. The more she twitched her tail, the closer it came to the fire. And then it was in the fire.

"Ouch!" she yelped. She darted away from the fireside clear across the room. The tip of her tail smoked.

"Ivy! That's it! You're a genius!" crowed Angus.

Ivy was trying desperately to regain her composure. "Of course, I am. What exactly did I do?"

"You reminded me of one time I went camping with my dad. He told me to bring my hiking boots but I didn't because they were stiff and uncomfortable. I told him that I'd packed them, but I actually brought my hi-tops instead."

Angus was crouching by the fire, arranging the rudimentary eyeglasses. He stopped talking as he fiddled with the crystals.

"Angus, you need to finish your story."

"What? Oh, yeah, sorry. So we went hiking on a really muddy trail and when we got back, my feet were wet. I propped my sneakers up against the campfire and they melted." He stared intently at the eyeglasses.

Ivy waited, and when it became clear that no other information was forthcoming, she prodded him. "What does that have to do with Granny's eyeglasses?"

"Well, it's obvious. The heat of the fire will soften the rubber and make it sticky. The goo will get on the crystals. When the rubber cools, the lenses will be stuck to the frame, and Granny will have her glasses. I do have to be careful not to melt the rubber or overheat the fluorite. Fluorite can crack when it's exposed to extreme changes in temperature."

He abruptly stopped talking and gasped. He nudged the glasses away from the fire with the end of his screwdriver and gaped at the lenses.

Ivy jumped to her feet, raised her hackles, and snarled. "Did you see that, Angus?"

The fluorite lenses were glowing violet.

"I've heard about this," said Angus. "We talked about thermoluminescence once in my Junior Rock Hounders club. I've never seen it before though."

"Explain."

"When a rock glows after it is heated, that's called thermoluminescence. What it means is that the rock releases energy it previously absorbed. That energy appears as light."

"But that's the exact same color of light as the large piece of crystal," began Ivy.

Angus was already pulling the World Jumper from his waistband and the large crystal from his pocket. He laid them on the floor side by side. The large crystal and Granny's glasses glowed the same shade of violet.

"But the large crystal hasn't been heated. Why is it glowing? And why is it that particular color?"

Angus stared at the crystals and shook his head. "I don't know."

26

Map Coordinates

Angus ran his fingers through his unruly brown hair. His three cowlicks exploded in different directions. He bounced excitedly on his toes as he paced the room, thinking out loud.

"The fluorite glows violet. Granny's glasses release the violet light when they are heated. The chunk glows when it's near the World Jumper even though it's not heated. The light is the energy that the rock had absorbed."

"Where does the energy come from?"

"From the location where the rock was. It picks up the surrounding energy."

"Why violet?"

"I don't know. Maybe it's the energy in the cave."

"Or in this world."

Angus stopped abruptly and stared at the dire wolf.

"What are you saying, Ivy?

"I followed your heat signature here. What is heat, but energy?"

Angus's eyes sparkled. "You think the violet glow is the energy of this world? Its heat signature. What if each world has a distinct energy? A very specific heat signature?"

Ivy watched him silently. He was on to something and she didn't want to interrupt.

Angus began pacing again. "The fluorite would glow a different color in every world. We would know what world we were on. But only if we'd been there before and had a color list. I wonder what color the pirate world is? Or home? What color is home?"

Ivy nodded toward the World Jumper. She was afraid to touch it with her wet nose. "How does it work?"

"I squeeze the trigger. A combination of moisture and baking soda activates it."

"Yes, I know that part. I mean, there are a lot of buttons on the front and that display screen. What do you do with those?"

Angus blinked. "I've never used those." He picked up the modified barcode scanner and examined it, carefully avoiding the trigger. The top half of the scanner was a blank display. The bottom half was a keypad of white letter buttons and red number buttons. Several gray buttons had functions assigned to them: Esc, Shift, Alt, Enter, Ctrl, and BkSp.

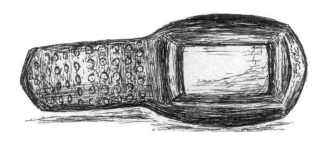

"I wonder."

"What?" prodded Ivy.

"The last time I jumped worlds, I tripped."

"So does that make you a World Tripper, not a World Jumper?" Ivy joked. "Sorry," she apologized as she caught Angus's evil glare. "Keep going."

"I grabbed the front of the scanner with my other hand. I probably pushed some buttons. Maybe that caused me to land here."

"If so, that combination of buttons could be the code for this world."

"Yes, like map coordinates." He looked at the scanner again, took a deep breath, pointed it at the crystal, and pulled the trigger.

"Angus, no!" yelled Ivy.

A red light blazed from the end of the scanner and reflected off the fluorite rock. The display of the barcode scanner lit up with the code 9F48C2.

Angus released the trigger and stood dumbfounded.

When several moments of silence had passed, Ivy could wait no longer. "What? What is it?"

"I think I just found the coordinates for this world." He looked at her. "We might be able to find our way home."

He looked around Billy's hut for an object he could use to test his theory. He pulled back a privacy curtain. A pallet and bedroll were crumpled into one corner and a week's worth of dirty socks lay in the other. He grinned. "Perfect." He pushed in the coordinates 9F48C2, pushed the Enter button, and pulled the World Jumper's trigger. Smoke puffed out the end.

"Careful, Angus! What are you doing?"

"It's okay. I'm programming the World Jumper. As long as I punch in the right coordinates and don't point it at myself, there's nothing to worry about."

The dire wolf poked her head around the curtain. Before she saw them, her keen nose detected the ripe, cheesy odor of sweaty socks. "Yuck! Billy's an even worse slob than you."

"I know. And I just zapped his socks."

"What happened?"

"Nothing. I used the coordinates of this world. They didn't move."

"Maybe your World Jumper's broken."

Angus shook his head. "No. It lit up and smoked. It's working. I wonder if this thing has a memory." He turned it and looked straight into the laser window.

"Careful! You're going to zap yourself!"

Uncharacteristically heeding her warning, Angus pointed the World Jumper at the socks again. "I remember a tiny computer chip when I took the scanner apart in my lab. I didn't get a chance to test it before I zapped myself. I wonder if it would have stored the other locations. And if it did, how do I access the memory?"

Ivy crept nervously toward him. "Tilt it up a bit so I can see." Angus complied, carefully moving his hand away from the sensitive trigger.

"Look at all those buttons!" said Ivy. "Exactly like a computer keyboard. You could type a story on there."

"Ivy! Once again, you amaze me! You are brilliant! Why didn't I think of that?"

"I don't know. I suggest fewer hours playing video games and more hours familiarizing yourself with your computer's word processing features. Or, maybe you're not in touch with your writing muse?"

Angus ignored her sarcastic comments. "See that Ctrl button? What happens on your computer if you push Ctrl-C?"

"You copy something."

"Ctrl-V?"

"You paste whatever you just copied. But how does that help us? You didn't copy or paste anything."

Angus was bouncing again. Ivy jumped back to avoid the World Jumper he was waving around recklessly in his excitement. "Put the World Jumper down, Angus, before there's another accident."

"Oh. Sorry." Angus placed the World Jumper gingerly on the floor beside Billy's pungent socks and tapped his foot impatiently. "What if you type something or delete something and then change your mind? What key combination do you use to get it back?"

"Ctrl-Z of course."

"Exactly!" Angus picked up the World Jumper again, pointed it carefully at the floor, and punched the buttons Ctrl, Z, Enter. The scanner buzzed and the code 1BBFE0 appeared on the screen. Angus tilted the World Jumper so Ivy could see it.

"If my theory is correct, that should be the exact location of the pirate world." He grinned mischievously. "Captain Hank and the crew should have just about finished cleaning the Fearsome Flea."

He pointed the scanner at Billy's socks, practically steaming with odor, and pulled the trigger. The World Jumper buzzed and smoked. The socks had disappeared.

Far away in a parallel world, a toothless pirate laid aside a mop and wiped the sweat from his brow. He bent backwards, hand supporting his lower back, and stretched his tight muscles.

"Aaargh. Thank Davey Jones me work's done," he sighed. He bent down to retrieve his mop and bucket of water. His toothless gums flapped open and shut with a wet smacking sound as he spotted the rancid woolen socks strewn across the Fearsome Flea's deck.

The dire wolf snarled and jumped back. Angus laughed happily.

"You can't be sure where those socks went," said Ivy.

"No, not unless I follow them. But since I've only used the World Jumper twice, it's a pretty safe bet that Billy's laundry will be walking the plank soon."

"Even if that's true, you still don't know the coordinates of your home world. You never programmed them into the scanner, so Ctrl-Z won't work."

"True," said Angus. He sighed and tucked the World Jumper back into his waistband. "We should leave before Billy's mother gets home." He tucked the rubber strips from the dismantled sneakers into his toolbelt. An inventor-in-training worth the title never throws away anything potentially useful.

He packed away his tools and jammed the large crystal into a compartment in his toolbelt between a tape measure and a ball of steel wool. Granny's glasses dangled from his fingertips. Ivy gathered the remnants of the purple sneakers in her mouth. The boy's shoulders slumping and the dire wolf's tail drooping, the two friends departed the hut.

27

Target Practice

Gus leaned on the window sill and gazed out. No monsters to guard against. No sloths to feed or tend. Not allowed to hunt. No forest to explore. No little sister to play with. What was he supposed to do all day? This hallucination was beginning to bore him. Maybe that meant he was getting better and would wake up soon?

He collapsed back on to the soft mattress. This dream bed was much more comfortable than his real one in the hut. But life in this dream home was terribly boring. What was the point of getting out of this bed?

"Mwowr."

Gus opened the door and looked down at the little monster, the *cat*. It trotted into his room as though it owned the place and Gus was only a visitor. It jumped onto the bed and curled up on the pillow. Gus watched it wash its face, yawn widely, and go to sleep. That was what happened here. Monsters got fat and lazy and fell asleep.

A terrible heaviness weighed on Gus's heart. He didn't like this hallucination. In this dream house, this dream village, his family had changed. They didn't even feel like his people. This house certainly didn't feel like home. Mother was always cleaning and tidying things. He didn't know where her loom had gone. Rather than do her handiwork, she sat idly looking at something called a *book*. She'd even gone so far as to tell him to go read one.

He'd thought it must be something truly fascinating, so he'd looked over her shoulder. It had been filled with strange symbols, like the ones the young villagers wore on their garments. The same symbols he'd seen at the store. He had grabbed the book from her hands and rifled through the pages. There was nothing in it except those symbols.

But if he thought his dream Mother's behavior was odd, Father's was utterly mind boggling. He sat staring at a tiny black box and touching it with his thumb. He called it a *smart phone*, probably because it took over his mind whenever he looked at it. Mother would call to him from across the room and he would jerk awake and say "Huh? What?" as he pulled his brain back from the box.

When he became tired with that, he went to another room and stared at another, larger black box. He called it a *computer*, and Father would watch it while his fingers moved clickety-clack across a *keyboard* covered in those strange symbols. Sometimes he would scratch his head as though he was confused and then his fingers would rat-a-tat the *keyboard*. Father would lean back in his chair and look very satisfied with himself.

Father had caught him watching and invited him to use a smaller *computer* to play a game. Gus had taken the cold, hard thing and examined it. He had wanted to play a game but he didn't understand how this box could play hide or hunt or chase with him. It had no legs and no arms, and he couldn't talk with it. All he wanted was Bonnie. He wanted to wake up.

One time he had asked Father if he could help to clean his weapons, his spear and hunting axe. Father had laughed, actually laughed at him, and told him to go and play. He had watched Mother capture a large black spider scrabbling along the floor. Rather than scream and squash it as she used to do, she gently released it out of doors. She even talked to it, telling it, "You don't belong in here. Go outside and eat some nasty bugs."

She yelled at him when he complimented her cooking with a booming belch. She yelled at him when he carried a pile of wood into the house.

(She said the *furnace* didn't burn wood.) She yelled at him when he fletched an arrow and whittled a bow. She put a pile of books in front of him, told him to *read*, and yelled at him when he built a slingshot instead. Dream Mother yelled all the time.

And never once did either of them mention Bonnie, his playmate, his sister.

"Angus! Breakfast!"

He heard her voice and dragged himself down the stairs. He didn't even feel like eating. On a normal day he would have been out of bed before dawn, caring for the sloths or hauling firewood. A steaming pot of stew would be waiting for him when he returned to the hut. Mother would be weaving or spinning while Bonnie wound yarn balls or played with a doll. If Father was home, he'd be sharpening weapons, repairing the hut, or helping the other men with a larger job. Granny would be organizing the village, training the older children, and making pottery. Gus missed the old village, the old life, his old family. Especially his sister.

"I've made sausage and grits," announced Mrs. Clark, grinning at him from beneath a faux coonskin cap. "Isn't that what they eat out on the trail? Yee haw!" She jumped in the air, attempting to click her cowboy boots together.

She placed a steaming bowl on the table. Gus had no idea what this was, but it smelled good. He took a bite. It was good.

"Yer paw is out the back, herdin' some cattle. Get along doggies!" She grabbed his empty bowl and pushed him out the door.

Father wore a balaclava, a camouflage vest, and Wellington boots over his blue jeans and t-shirt. He waved a coil of rope over his head and tossed it at a fence post. "Let's rope these cows!" he yelled when he saw Gus.

Gus looked around the small suburban yard. Except for a curious black crow gazing down from the safety of a branch and a chittering gray squirrel, there were no animals to be seen. What cows was Father talking about?

"Or would you rather go on safari? Hunt some lions and tigers with a bow and arrow?" Father dropped the rope and picked up a large bow. He nocked an arrow and aimed at a large round foam circle positioned against the fence on the other side of the yard. "That's an elephant!" announced Father as he loosed the arrow.

His aim was as bad as Granny's and the arrow sailed over the fence and into the neighbor's yard. "What are you doing over there, Clark? You could have put someone's eye out!" yelled an angry voice.

"Sorry. Just toss it back over the fence."

Gus heard a crack, and two pieces of arrow flew back into the Clark's yard.

"Want to try? Shoot the elephant?" Father handed the bow to Gus.

Gus looked at the foam painted with concentric circles of red, green, and blue. "That's an *elephant*?" he asked.

"Sure. That's an elephant. Or it could be a giraffe or hippo or rhino. What do you want it to be?"

"What is it?"

"Well, obviously it's a target. You can pretend it's anything you want. Then you can be a hunter and kill it."

"Why would I do that? Can we eat it?"

"It's made of foam, Angus. I mean Gus. Of course, we can't eat it."

"Then why would I kill it? Is it dangerous? Would it kill us?"

"If you want it to, I guess you could pretend it's dangerous."

"But is it? Really? I don't want to hurt it if we can't eat it and it's not going to hurt us."

"Angus, Gus, it's a piece of foam! Just shoot it!"

"Why?"

"Your mother says we have to play. You want to be a hunter, don't you? Just shoot it."

"Oh, are you trying to train me for the mammoth hunt? Do you think I'm old enough? Can I go next time?"

"Mammoth, dinosaur, bigfoot, I don't care. Just shoot it!"

Gus nocked an arrow, sighted the target, pulled the bow string, and released. The arrow whistled through the air and hit the bullseye.

Father whooped. "Great shot! Want to try again?"

"Yes, sir." Gus aimed and fired. The second arrow hit the center again and sliced into the first.

"Whoa! Fantastic, son! Why don't you step back ten feet and see how you do?"

Gus increased his distance from the target and tried again. The arrow sunk into the target a millimeter away from the first two.

Mr. Clark raised his hand in the air. "High five!" he announced.

Gus looked at his father's outstretched hand and put the bow into it. "Spear next?" Gus asked.

28

Discovery Beneath the Hut

"What do you mean you haven't seen her all day?"

"Just what I said. I've been working on these for Granny." Angus proudly presented the sneaker rubber and fluorite eyeglasses to Gus's grandmother.

Granny examined the offering with interest. "Like this Granny," said Angus as he tied the rubber frames around her head with a shoelace from the purple sneakers.

"Well, who was watching her?" continued Mother, growing more anxious with every passing moment.

Granny gasped and spun around the room. "Gus! What have you done!"

Angus looked at her fearfully and stammered, "Sorry, Granny. I'll take them off."

"You'll do no such thing, young man!" She focused two gigantic eyes on him. "You'll come right over here and give your Granny a hug. I haven't seen this well since, since, ever! Those woodland creatures don't stand a chance! We'll have squirrel stew, squirrel pie, squirrel soup, roast squirrel for every meal!" She wrapped her arms around him and squeezed. She kissed the top of his head and released him. "I can't wait to go hunting! Where's my bow and arrow?"

"Hasn't anyone heard a thing I've said?" interrupted Mother. "Where is Bonnie?"

"Bonnie? Has that fool girl gone missing again?" asked Granny.

"Gus, you're supposed to mind your sister when I'm away," said Mother.

"Oh, leave off the boy. He has other things to do besides watch that girl. She is old enough to follow the rules."

What was this? Granny was taking Angus's side? He guessed she liked those glasses.

"He needs to help when his father is away. I can't run this family alone," said Mother.

"And I suppose I do nothing to help? You're doing it all alone, are you?" said Granny.

"That's not what I said. You're always misunderstanding me. And anyway, for once this isn't about you. It's about Bonnie and where she is."

"There you go again. Thinking I make everything about me. Honestly! Who was it went up to the plateau the last time you lost your kids?"

"I didn't lose my kids! And I thanked you for that. But that doesn't change the fact that Bonnie is missing and no one knows where she is."

"And I suppose somehow that's my fault too. Blame everything on the old lady."

"That's not what I said! If you would listen for once!"

Angus heard an insistent barking from outside the family's yurt. Granny and Mother were becoming so focused on each other and their disagreement that neither noticed him slip out the doorway.

"What's wrong, Ivy?"

"I knew I smelled cat! I told you. Come and look!"

The dire wolf trotted around the side of the yurt. She lay in the snow and pointed her muzzle at a gap below the house. "There. I can smell it in there."

Angus lay down beside her and peered into the dark space. "I don't see anything. It's too dark."

He poked through his toolbelt until he located the little penlight. He switched it on and off, banged it against his palm, and switched it on again. The batteries were definitely dead. He pulled out the World Jumper. Careful not to press the buttons, he aimed it under the hut and pulled the trigger. A red light flashed and Angus saw two eyes glowing back at him in the darkness beneath the hut. He caught his breath and nearly dropped the World Jumper.

"There's something in there!" he said.

"I know. It smells like cat."

"Oh. That's not so bad. I have a cat at home. I know what to do."

Angus spoke into the gap. "Here, kitty. Come out, kitty." He made squeaking noises with his lips. A tiny mew reached his ears. The eyes drew nearer. Angus continued sweet-talking until a tiny orange-brown head poked through the opening and amber eyes peeked up at him. They flickered over his shoulder and the cat hissed. Angus turned and saw the dire wolf panting eagerly.

"Ivy, go away!" Angus shoved at her shoulder. A large gob of drool dropped from her gaping mouth and landed on his hand. He wiped it in the snow and glared at her. She lowered her ears and backed off.

He turned his attention back to the cat. He squeaked and called until it ventured out again. This time he scooped it in his arms and stood up. He stroked its ears and coaxed out a soft rumbling purr. "You're a little bigger than my cat, Sir Schnortle. But you act like a kitten." The cat gazed at him with trusting eyes, reached out a soft paw, and jabbed at his cheek.

"That's not a housecat," called Ivy's voice from the other side of the hut. "It's a lion cub. I can smell it."

Angus peered at the animal curled in his arms. "Yes, I think you are a lion cub. A very young one. What are you doing beneath our house?"

"Bonnie," came the dire wolf's voice.

"You think that's what she's been up to?"

"Yes. And if she's got the lion cub, we've got a problem."

"Meaning?"

"There's one very unhappy mama looking for her stolen baby."

The lion cub stiffened in Angus's arms as the argument inside the yurt grew louder.

"Make that two unhappy mothers," said Angus.

29

Back to the Cave

Concealing the lion cub in his heavy fur coat, Angus pushed back the drape and peered into the hut. He interrupted the quarreling women. "Ivy and I are going to look for Bonnie before it gets dark."

"That's what I've been saying! I'll go, too," said Mother.

"No, no. You stay here in case she comes back. I'll go with Gus. Now that I can see, I'll be a better shot than you," said Granny.

Angus cringed. He couldn't let that happen. Granny couldn't go with him! He had to get the lion cub back to its den. She'd ruin everything.

"Granny, I have Ivy with me. She's a good tracker. How about we search the forest and you search the village?"

"Not a chance, young man! Pet or no, that area is far too dangerous for you this late in the day. But splitting up is a good suggestion. I'll take the forest, and you and Ivy can search the village."

"But—"

"Now that's the end of it, or you can stay here and wait for Bonnie and I'll take your mother with me instead."

Angus reached for the spear propped against the wall.

"You won't need that in the village," said Granny. "Now, take your wolf and go look for Bonnie."

Angus scowled. There was no arguing with Granny. She was right; no need for a spear in the village. Of course, he had no intention of staying in the village but insisting on the spear would make her suspicious. He grabbed the snowshoes as he left the house. The dire wolf was nowhere to be seen.

"Ivy! Ivy!" he called.

"Up here," answered a creaky high-pitched voice from the roof of the yurt. A huge bird with a bald head, crooked neck, and bulging eyes looked down at him.

Angus cringed. "Yuck. A vulture, Ivy? Really?"

"Shows what you know," cackled the hideous fowl. "I'm a teratorn. *Teratornis merriami* to be exact. Nearly twice the size of a California Condor. But essentially a vulture, yes."

Far above them both, Angus saw an assembly of the gruesome birds circling over the meat hut. They cast ominous, dark shadows on the ground. Ivy coasted down beside Angus.

I saw that kettle of teratorns over there and thought: What better animal to scan an area from a distance? The lion won't be able to surprise us this time."

Angus sat in a snow bank and fastened the snowshoes to his boots. "Granny says I can't leave the village."

"She always says you can't leave the village. Hasn't stopped you yet."

"I'll have to get out another way."

"I thought of that already." The ugly bird flapped her wings and glided through the village. "Follow me."

Angus jogged along behind Ivy to the far end of the village. She continued flying over the mammoth bone fence and landed softly in the snow on the other side. She squawked in frustration as her talons sunk into the pristine powder.

"Under the fence. Last thing I did before leaving the dire wolf body."

A wide ditch had been dug beneath the fence and ended in wolf tracks leaving the village. Angus peeked into a small opening in his coat and reassured the young animal hidden there.

"We're going to take you home. This next bit will be a little rough." He tucked in the lion cub before sliding through the hole. The cub protested mildly but settled down once Angus was upright again.

"Granny will be in the forest looking for Bonnie," said Angus. "How do we get up to the plateau without her seeing me?"

"Don't you remember how we got down last time? We'll follow the mastodon trail around the side and scale the cliffs."

"Easy for you to say! You can fly there. I'll have to climb up all those rocks!"

"You climbed up the side of the Fearsome Flea with a rope attached to a screwdriver. Rocks will be easy."

"Yeah, true. But this time I have the added weight of a lion cub." He patted his coat.

Ivy pulled one bony foot out of the snow and pointed it at Angus. "What do you think these talons are for? I can haul the cub up the cliff."

Angus wrapped his arms protectively around the large lump in the front of his coat. "No way are you sinking those things into this little guy!" A tiny muffled mew agreed with him.

Ivy flapped her expansive wings and took off. "Just trying to help. The trail is this way."

Angus leaned panting against a large boulder at the bottom of the ravine. He had jogged nearly the entire way trying to keep up with the hideous teratorn and outpace the afternoon sun.

"Why don't you rest for a few minutes? I'll fly up to the plateau and see what's going on."

"Great idea." Angus stretched his leg muscles and gazed up at the white sky. No trace of the beautiful blue sky that had started the day. But no threatening gray clouds either, so that was good. He reached into his coat and touched the cub's furry head. It squeaked faintly. He must have woken it from a cat nap. It nuzzled in closer to him and sighed as it absorbed his body heat.

Angus removed his snowshoes and strapped them to his back. He started up the slope. He took his time, picking out flat areas, grasping rocks, and hauling himself painfully up the hill. He stopped frequently to catch his breath and gauge his progress. He was slow but steady and had made his way halfway up the slope when a dark shadow alerted him that Ivy had returned. She glided down and landed on a boulder.

"Angus."

Something in her voice alarmed him. He grabbed hold of a jutting stone to steady himself and looked at her.

"Granny is up there. She found something. A trail of crystals. They stopped at the end of the forest."

"A trail of them?"

Ivy nodded. "Like someone put them there on purpose."

"How do you know?"

"Granny talks to herself. Out loud. She's going back to the village to get help."

Angus waited, not quite understanding.

"She thinks Bonnie left them."

"Did you see her footprints up there?"

"Snowshoe prints."

"They can't be from her." He motioned to the snowshoes strapped to his back. "She didn't steal my snowshoes and she doesn't have her own pair. I made those prints yesterday. Anything else?"

"Lion."

"So she can't be up there. It's not possible."

"What are you carrying in your coat?" asked Ivy.

"My toolbelt. The World Jumper."

"Anything else?" Ivy pressed.

"Do you mean the lion cub?"

The teratorn looked grave. Angus stared. "Are you saying you think the mother lion carried Bonnie all the way up there the same way I'm carrying her cub?"

"I don't know why she wouldn't have eaten her right away, but yes, that's what I think."

Angus felt sick. He collapsed against the side of the hill. "Poor kid." He sat motionless for a few minutes, and then he stood. He grabbed the jutting stone and pulled his body up.

"Where are you going, Angus? What can you possibly do?"

"Granny doesn't know how to get into the cave. She doesn't even know there is a cave. It could be an hour at the very least before she's back from the village with help. If Bonnie has any chance at all it will be because her big brother is brave enough to face a lion."

30

The Crystal Lair

With a final, exhausted groan, Angus pulled himself to the top of the cliff. He rolled on to his back in the snow and sucked air. A fuzzy brown head poked out the top of his coat and nuzzled his chin with a wet nose. He stroked it until the lion cub began to purr.

"I've scanned the area and can't find the lion." The teratorn swooped down beside him. "Maybe she's under cover of the trees in the forest."

Ivy didn't say the lion could also be in the cave. That was understood by both of them. There would be no way to know the truth until Angus was inside. It would be too late then.

"I have to go into the cave. If the lion is gone and Bonnie is there, I can help her escape."

"And if the lion's there?"

"Can't you jump into its body?"

Ivy thought about this. "I have to see the animal to body jump. I can't go into the cave as a teratorn. If the lion is in the cave—wait a second."

The hideous bird took to the sky and flew toward the forest. Angus watched it depart. He became alarmed when it continued on without stopping. It became smaller and smaller in the distance until it was only a gray speck on the horizon.

"Where is she going?" Angus asked the amber eyes.

"She's right here," squeaked the lion cub. "Take me out of your coat as soon as you reach the cave entrance. If the mother lion is there, I'll body jump right away."

"And we can rescue Bonnie." He didn't say: If she's still alive. He felt in his heart that she must be. He didn't want to consider the alternative. He pushed Ivy down snugly into his coat.

Angus slapped on his snowshoes and hurried across the plateau. He reached the boulders that hid the cave entrance. He was pulling off the snowshoes when he heard a high-pitched snarl. His head whipped around to face that of an aggressive lion just leaving the cave.

"Let me out! I can't jump if I can't see her!" Ivy's voice was muffled.

Angus fumbled with his coat but the mother lion was on him in seconds. She made a soft, snorting sound. She mouthed his fur coat gently and began tugging him into the cave opening. Ivy nudged hard at the top of his coat. Her head poked through into the open air and the mother lion released Angus.

"I'm here," said the cave lion.

"That was close," said Angus. He stood up in the crystal cave and brushed snow and dirt from his clothes.

"No. I don't think it was," said Ivy. "Go ahead and let the cub out."

As Angus released the little animal from his coat, Ivy explained. "Those vocalizations she made weren't aggressive. They were friendly sounds. Like she knew you and was welcoming you to her lair."

"Pet!" yelled a familiar voice. Angus looked toward the rear of the cave. Bonnie scooped up the cub and cradled it in her arms.

Angus ran to the little girl and wrapped his arms around her. "Bonnie! You're safe!"

She pushed him away. "Of course I'm safe."

"You're in a lion's den. Its lair." Angus spread his arms wide. "This is the crystal lair of the monster. Do you know how worried everyone is? Granny is on her way up here with a group of villagers to rescue you."

"Rescue? I don't need to be rescued." Bonnie cooed at the cub and petted its head.

"You went off without telling anyone. You're lucky you weren't killed!"

"You sound like Granny and Mommy."

"I do not!" Okay, maybe he did, a little. But when you love someone, you worry about them. He shook his head to get that awful thought out of there. Love the little pest? No way! "Why didn't you tell me you had found a lion cub?"

"You have a pet. I want my own pet."

"Bonnie, the animal you chose for a pet was someone else's baby," said Ivy. "The lion cub has a mother, and when you took it, you upset her."

"Whoa! The lion mommy can talk!" said Bonnie. She reached out a hand and stroked Ivy's head.

Angus scowled. "Aren't you afraid of her?"

Bonnie ignored him and skipped around the cave, chattering and pointing out bright crystals to the purring lion cub.

Angus shook his head and watched the silly little girl. "I don't get it."

"Angus, I can't see."

He looked at the cave lion. "What?"

"I can see shapes and dim lights but nothing is clear. I can sort of make out that you're standing there but I can't tell that you're Angus. Not with my eyes. And you smell like cat. Probably because you've been carrying that lion cub all day."

"Can you see Bonnie or the lion cub? They're over there." He pointed to the right side of the cave.

"Moving blurs. That's all I see. I can smell them. But I can't tell them apart by smell."

Angus began pacing. He traipsed back and forth while he considered what Ivy had told him.

"When you're in an animal's body, you experience everything that animal feels, right?"

"Yes."

"So tell me everything. What is your body feeling?"

"Hungry. My stomach is empty. Weak. Lack of energy. A little achy, like I got punched everywhere."

"Ivy, when you were a dire wolf you thought something was wrong with the lion. That was the reason you were able to survive your fight with it. It was weak and thin. Now that you're in the lion body, you say you can't see. Do you think that's why this lion was hunting the corralled sloths? They were easy to find and to kill?"

"That definitely makes sense," said Ivy. "A half-blind lion can't hunt fast moving animals. And with a lion cub to feed, she would have been desperate for food."

"But how do you explain her not killing and eating Bonnie? If she's so hungry, a small child would have been an easy meal."

"If she realized Bonnie was human."

"What do you mean?"

"Angus, I told you I can't see. The blind have to rely on their other senses. Taste, touch, smell, hearing. Bonnie smells like a lion cub. With her fur coat, she feels like a lion cub. If I think she might be a lion cub, I'm not going to taste her."

"What about hearing? The minute she speaks, she's no longer a lion cub."

"Are you Gus?"

"No. I'm Angus."

"But Mother doesn't know that. You look like Gus. Your voice sounds like his. But you're not Gus. Bonnie noticed right away. Probably some part of Mother knows you're not Gus, but she needs to love a boy, and you're enough like her son that she accepts you as him. The mother lion needs to love her cub. Bonnie is close enough, so she took her."

Angus nodded. "It's an interesting theory. That would explain why Bonnie's not afraid. The mother lion took her and Bonnie thought she was another pet. It's a big game to her. She's playing with cats. But now it's time to leave. I have to get Bonnie out of here, and then you have to jump into another animal."

"You can't leave the lion like this!" protested Ivy. "She has a baby to care for and she can barely feed herself. They'll both die if we do nothing. And don't forget Granny is on her way with her new eyeglasses and an army. The cave lion doesn't stand a chance."

"What do you suggest?" asked Angus.

"Eyeglasses."

"Excuse me?"

"Eyeglasses for the lion."

"You're joking. That's ridiculous," said Angus.

"Why not? Think about it. We're surrounded by crystal. If the lion can see, there will be no reason for her to stay here and eat stinky sloth. She can follow the mastodon, hunt camels. She'll have options. You'll be doing her, the cub, and the village a service."

Angus stared into space. Then he moved to one of the sparkling walls. He adjusted his safety goggles, and rifled through his toolbelt and pulled out a hammer and chisel. He pried several clear crystals from the wall. He knelt and spread the crystals over the cave floor. He checked them for size and aberrations. The World Jumper tucked into his waistband was uncomfortable, so he set it on the ground too. He tucked the hammer and chisel away and began searching through his toolbelt.

"I'm sure I put some in here," he said to himself.

"What are you looking for?" asked Ivy.

"I know I put some of the sneaker rubber in here. But there's so much other stuff in here now." He felt the cold, hard surface of the large crystal and pulled it out. He put it on the ground and continued looking for the rubber. "Here it is! I knew I'd find it!"

He held the rubber strips to the cave lion's head. "This isn't going to work, Ivy. Your head is wider than a human head. And your ears aren't on the side of your face. They're on the top of your head."

"Think Angus, fast. Granny's on her way, remember?"

Angus stood up and began pacing.

"Where are you going, Angus?"

"Nowhere. Moving helps me think." He paced to the other side of the cave, ran his fingers along the wall, and then he turned and walked back to the original side where the cave lion waited. He turned again and had walked half the distance to the other side of the cave before he started bouncing. "That's it! I'll finally have a chance to make the Cat Muffler! Well, part of it anyhow."

"What's that?" asked Ivy.

Angus hurried back to her, stripped off his coat, thick wool sweater, and hand-woven undershirt. He shivered, and quickly put the sweater and coat back on. He talked the entire time.

"It's an invention I designed in my lab. My cat, Sir Schnortle, makes terrible noises at night. I designed the Cat Muffler to, well, muffle him. We won't need the entire thing, because we're not trying to muffle you, the lion. We only need the head gear, and only part of that. It doesn't need to cover your entire head, just your eyes.

"The problem is that I don't have a piece of rubber large enough. All I have is this shirt and it won't last forever. I mean, Ivy, this isn't a zoo. Whatever I make for the lion is going to fall apart at some point, that is, if the lion even tolerates it. My cat won't let me put anything on his head."

"I know. But we have to at least try."

"So my idea is that I put the crystals into the rubber like I did for Granny. I cut my shirt to fit over your ears and wrap around your head. Like a cap. Then I attach the rubber eyeglass piece to the bottom of that."

"How are you going to keep it from falling off when the lion runs? A shirt will be loose and billowy."

"I already used the shoelaces for Granny's glasses," said Angus. He looked at the leather straps wrapped around his boots. He unstrung them, wrapped them lightly around Ivy's head, and pronounced them adequate.

He was glad he had cut the rubber strips at Billy's house. One was barely long enough to stretch between the lion's eyes. Now he only needed to make the X's for the crystals to rest in. A few slashes with the stolen knife made short work of the job.

Next out of his toolbelt was a book of matches that he had "forgotten" to return to his father after helping him to start a campfire last summer. He lit one after another and held them to the rubber as long as he could. He only singed his fingers twice. With only two matches to spare, he assessed the violet glowing crystals to be sufficiently glued.

Next, he turned his attention to the undershirt. He draped it on top of the cave lion's head, measured the distance from ear to ear, and then cut earholes with the knife. He shortened the head covering to lie right below the eyes and cut a long opening for the rubber strip. He slipstitched the rubber strip to the shirt—thanks to Mom for teaching him to sew that winter he explored taxidermy as a possible career.

"Are you ready to try it on?" he asked the uncharacteristically motionless Ivy crouching beside him. He was reminded of Sir Schnortle who would wait patiently until his chase toy was directly over his nose before reaching out a lazy paw to catch it.

"Yes."

He put the covering over the cave lion's head, one ear through each hole, the crystals perfectly aligned over each eye. A contented motor rumbled to life. "Much better," purred Ivy.

"Now to secure it so it won't fall off," said Angus, wrapping the leather ties around the base of her ears, over the top of her head, and along the ridgeline of her jaw. "Tight enough? Or too tight?"

"A little tighter on the head, a little looser on my face."

When Ivy pronounced the eyeglasses a comfortable fit, she bounded around the cave, shook her head, and swiped at the head covering with a large paw.

"What are you doing? You'll break it!" said Angus.

"What do you think the lion is going to do once she gets her body back? I want to be sure she can't get it off. Hey, Angus. I'm not sure these eyeglasses are totally working."

"What do you mean? Is your vision blurry?"

"No. But I'm not sure about the color distortion."

"That violet glow will fade once the energy in the rock dissipates."

"No, that doesn't bother me. But it looks like the large crystal, the one on the floor next to your World Jumper, is green. Nothing else has a green glow, so I'm just wondering—"

Angus looked at his World Jumper. He hadn't realized he'd put it right next to the crystal again. This time, rather than violet, the crystal was glowing green. Angus grabbed the World Jumper off the floor and the crystal became clear again. Angus touched the World Jumper to the crystal once more. Green.

"I have to check this out," said Angus. He pointed the scanner at the large crystal chunk and pulled the trigger. The display read 2BE01B.

"What does it say?" asked Ivy.

"A different code from the other two we had." He pointed the World Jumper at the cave wall and pulled the trigger. The display read 9F48C2. Those were the coordinates of this world. Violet.

"The energy isn't coming from the cave. I think it's from another world."

"But doesn't fluorite pick up energy from its surroundings?"

"Yes."

"So how did that piece of fluorite pick up energy from a green world if we're still in the violet one?"

"I don't know." Angus picked up the crystal and juggled it in his hand. He stuck it back into his toolbelt.

"Wait a minute! Did you have that crystal in your toolbelt this whole time?"

"Yeah. It's a lot more comfortable carrying it in there than jamming it into my pocket."

"Is that toolbelt from your home world?"

"You know it is. Why are you asking? Oh." Angus was silent. He stared at Ivy, and then slumped against the crystal wall.

Could it really be that easy? His toolbelt was from home. Could the crystal have picked up that energy? If he merely programmed the World Jumper with those coordinates, could he finally return home?

"Bonnie! Where are you? Bonnie!" The faint sound of voices drifted into the cave.

Ivy looked toward the cave entrance through her new eyeglasses. "They're here."

31

Green

"Bonnie, you need to go. Quickly," said Angus.

Bonnie gripped the lion cub tightly. The little animal squeaked against her chest and squirmed away. It ran to the cave lion and rubbed its body up against its mother, purring loudly.

"I want to take my pet."

"Bonnie, it's not your pet. It's a wild lion cub. It needs its mother. It needs to learn to be a lion. It will grow into a large predator, too big and too dangerous to live with you in the village. Besides, Granny and the others will kill it."

"No!" wailed the little girl. "Pet is my friend!"

Ivy spoke. "Bonnie, Pet's mother will be killed if the villagers see her. And Pet wants to be with her mother. Do you want your friend's mother to die?"

"No." Bonnie kicked at the ground.

"If you love Pet, you need to leave her with her mother," said Angus. "You need to go so Granny and the others don't find the cave. This cave is our secret, right? No one else can know about it."

Bonnie nodded silently. She reached out and stroked the cub. "Bye, Pet." She walked to the cave opening, peered out, and scrambled through.

Angus exhaled loudly. "Now what? Should we try this new code? See where it takes us?"

"Angus, think. If you jump worlds right now, Gus is going to wind up inside this cave face-to-face with me. Only, he won't realize I'm a girl in the body of a cave lion. He's going to see a fierce predator."

"Yeah, right. Not such a good plan."

"Plus, do you really think Bonnie is going to stay away from this cave? There are sparkling crystals, a cute little lion cub, and she's not afraid of the lion. But the next time, the cave lion is going to be able to see her, smell that she's human, and react like a protective mother lion."

"Not good."

"No. Definitely not good."

"Got any ideas?"

"I have to take this lion body and this lion cub far away. Now that she can see, mother lion has no need to hunt sloth. We have to get her down on the game trail."

"You mean on the trail at the bottom of the ravine?"

"Exactly. She can hunt the mastodon or follow the trail wherever it leads. Get out of this forested area.

They heard whooping shouts outside the cave. "Bonnie! You're alive!"

Angus smiled at Ivy. "As soon as they leave, we'll get you well on your way."

Angus had to admit it. The kid was good. Bonnie had feigned hunger and complained of the cold. She had whined until the search party had agreed to take her back to the village immediately. Granny had suggested she and a few others remain to search the plateau for the monster's hideaway, but Bonnie had convinced them that the monster had a secret path through the forest and was out hunting. She had suggested that it might even be on its way to the village and the sloth corral. The lack of fresh snow made it impossible for the trackers to determine in which direction the monster had gone.

The final decision had come from Mother. She had snatched Granny's eyeglasses from her face and refused to give them back until they reached the safety of the village.

"Just because you can see doesn't mean you're a match for that monster."

"Now I'm too old to protect my family?"

"It has nothing to do with your age. It's a monster. You need a hunting party, not a group of boys and their mothers."

"So we're a bunch of weaklings, are we?"

"That's not what I said!"

Angus and Ivy listened at the entrance to the cave until they could no longer hear Mother and Granny bickering. Angus poked his head through the opening. "All clear."

Ivy plunked the lion cub outside and then crawled through. She nipped the scruff of the cub's neck and trotted across the plateau toward the ravine. She turned her head back and looked at him through her headgear before she went over the cliff and was gone. Angus checked his gear. His safety goggles were on the top of his head, toolbelt around his waist, World Jumper in his clenched fist. He trudged across the plateau to the cover of the forest, found himself a log, and sat down to wait.

Angus was glad to be wrapped in fur. It was cold. He pulled the coat tighter around his body and it occurred to him that his alter ego, Gus, would be wearing the clothing of whatever world he'd been vaulted into when Angus jumped into this one. He was unlikely to be wearing furs.

Angus began trekking down the mountain toward the village. He didn't want to strand the guy on the plateau in the cold at nightfall. By the time he reached the bottom, the overcast sky had turned dusky. Just as he began thinking Ivy would not know where to find him, a gigantic rodent jumped into his arms.

"Yaaarrr!" he yelled, jumping to his feet and propelling the furry creature into the air.

"Skirreee!" A cat-sized squirrel scolded him. "It's me!"

"Sorry, you startled me. Have you seen yourself? You look like a giant rat!"

"Do not. I've got a bushy tail, see?" She waggled it at him.

"How'd it go?"

"I got her down the trail several miles past the village. When I smelled a herd of mastodon, I jumped into a bird. She pawed at the head gear a few times, and then gave up. I think she'll be fine."

"I hope so." He held up the World Jumper. "Are we going to try this thing?"

"We've got nothing to lose."

"Are you going to jump with me? Should we try a double jump?"

Ivy fluffed her tail between two agile paws. "Let's see if this body can jump with you. A double jump would save me some trouble." She scratched behind her ear. "If we don't end up back in your home world, let's at least hope for a world with flea powder." Ivy climbed into his lap.

"Here goes nothing," said Angus. He programmed 2BE01B and pressed Enter. He took a deep breath, pointed the World Jumper at himself, and pulled the trigger.

Granny, Mother, and Bonnie sat huddled around the fire. Mother had been so happy to have her little girl back that it had not occurred to her until dinner, when Gus ceased to appear, that she was now missing her other child.

"I told him not to leave the village. Ordered him!" Granny noticed a flicker in Bonnie's eyes. "What is it child? You know something. Where is he?"

"Oh, please! He can't be on the plateau! Is he up there, all alone? Tell us!" Mother grabbed Bonnie's shoulders.

Cold air gusted into the hut. A shivering and confused boy wearing a shirt covered in strange symbols stood blinking in the firelight. Bonnie scrambled to her feet and ran at him. She knocked him to the ground crying, "Gus! Gus! Gusseee!"

He wrapped his arms around her, kissed the top of her head, and breathed, "Bonnie."

She closed her eyes and smiled. "You're back."

Angus grabbed his head and willed the spinning to stop. He didn't think he'd ever get used to the dizziness and disorientation of jumping between worlds.

Despite the buzzing in his head, his body was surprisingly relaxed. He rested on a soft, yet firm, surface. His head was nestled on something cool and fluffy. A gentle swish-swishing was the only sound he heard. A familiar, but not entirely pleasant, smell tickled his nose. He flared his nostrils, and then he rubbed his nose with a finger. It almost smelled like paint.

Angus opened his eyes and sat up. A glaring, painful light nearly blinded him. He squinted his eyes and peered through his fingers.

A fierce, hungry black panther gaped at him.

Angus opened his eyes a little more and tried to back away slowly, but he was stopped by a— wall?

He was leaning against a wall with a painting of a pirate ship. Now that his eyes had adjusted to the light, he realized that the panther was also a painting.

He looked down at the bed he was sitting on. He reached over the side and turned off the giant shop light that had momentarily blinded him. And then he saw the back side of a woman who looked like Mom. She ignored him as she finished the brush strokes on a cactus in a Wild West scene on one of the four painted walls.

Angus let out a dejected sigh. He had been so hopeful. He thought he'd finally figured out how the World Jumper worked. This room looked a lot like his, but he didn't have paintings all over the walls, a superhero comforter, and a tent pitched in the corner. His mother didn't wear a cowboy hat and chaps. And she certainly didn't paint.

Well, maybe this world was more normal, more like his home world, more comfortable than the other worlds he'd arrived in. He'd have to wait until Ivy found him.

Apparently, the double jump hadn't worked because there was no sign of a squirrel—only a fat orange cat with a splotch of blue paint on his head.

Acknowledgments

Thank you to my cheering squad at Chestnut Hill Academy. Christi and Lisa, you introduced Angus to your bright, young students, and I thank you. Their need to know more about Angus and Ivy kept me writing.

Thank you to my informal marketing team. Mom and Dad, Kathy, and Ellen, your faith in me is overwhelming.

Thank you to my eagle-eyed editor, Leslie Cole. I continue to learn so much about written expression from you.

Thank you to my hilarious and creative illustrator, Jennifer Hotes. If anyone is Angus's doting aunt, you are.

Thank you to my supportive husband, Matt. It takes all kinds of patience to listen to me worry about a boy who exists in my head.

And thank you, Aidan, for sharing me with Angus.

D.M. DARROCH thinks there is no more beautiful sound than the laughter of children. She spent her childhood in western New York and was educated at American University and at Thunderbird School of Global Management.

She always wanted to write for a living and has penned newspaper feature articles, written software guides, and worked as a translator. Now she loves writing for children.

You may meet her on a hiking trail in the beautiful Pacific Northwest where she lives with her husband, her son, and two opinionated felines.

Learn more at www.dmdarroch.com.

JENNIFER L. HOTES was raised across the river from the Hanford Nuclear Reactor and grew up looking at the world a little differently. Now she uses her unique perspective and glow-in-the-dark countenance to write YA novels and illustrate for many talented authors.

Mrs. Hotes loves living in the rainy Pacific Northwest, volunteering in her children's schools and helping raise funds for Providence Hospice of Seattle.